Kidsboro

THE RISKY REUNION

by Marshal Younger

from Adventures in Odyssey®

Tyndale House Publishers, Inc.

Carol Stream, Illinois

A Focus on the Family book published by
Tyndale House Publishers, Inc., Carol Stream, Illinois 60188

Focus on the Family, Adventures in Odyssey, and *Kidsboro* and their accompanying logos and designs are trademarks of Focus on the Family, Colorado Springs, CO 80995.

TYNDALE and Tyndale's quill logo are registered trademarks of Tyndale House Publishers, Inc.

Editor: Kathy Davis
Cover design by Joseph Sapulich
Cover illustration © 2008 by Rob Johnson. All rights reserved.

Library of Congress Cataloging-in-Publication Data
Younger, Marshal.
  The risky reunion / Marshal Younger.
    p. cm. — (Kidsboro ; 4)
  Summary: With difficulty, Kidsboro mayor Ryan Cummings gets an annual budget passed but soon nearly everyone in town is unhappy, due either to the high taxes they are expected to pay, or to the services on which their money is being spent.
  ISBN-13: 978-1-58997-412-8
  ISBN-10: 1-58997-412-3
  [1. Politics, Practical—Fiction. 2. Municipal finance—Fiction. 3. Conduct of life—Fiction. 4. Christian life—Fiction.] I. Title.
  PZ7.Y8943Riu 2007
  [Fic]—dc22

                                    2007009636

Printed in the United States of America
1 2 3 4 5 6 7 8 9 /13 12 11 10 09 08

For Kristyn,
my third-born.
I can still make you laugh
at any given moment,
even though I haven't come up with
any new jokes since 2003.
I wish more people were like you.

● ● ●

ONE

A REALLY BAD PARADE

I PRESSED MY LIPS tightly together and tried to force the laughter from my ears. It was worse than when I thought of something funny during church. I glanced over and noticed that Scott Sanchez, my best friend, was about to burst as well. I exchanged covert smiles with Nelson Swanson and Jill Segler. Alice Funderburk, the only member of the Kidsboro city council who was taking this performance seriously, was listening intently.

The Clean Up Kidsboro group continued their presentation, as passionate about the environment as they could be. Mark was the leader of the group of three, and he dramatically pulled a prop out of a garbage bag. It was a picture of a large, ripe, perfect pumpkin. The picture was on a stand, and he propped it up on the table.

"This," Mark said, "is the human lung." Scott snickered at the thought. I had no idea what Mark meant. Mark reached back into the bag and pulled out an actual pumpkin, cut in half so we could see the inside. We turned our noses away in unison. It was rotted out and black with fungus. He placed it on the table next to the picture. "This," Mark continued, "is the human lung after it has been exposed to just two weeks of air pollution. Disgusting, isn't it?" He was right. I'd never be able to eat pumpkin pie again.

Mark went on. "Pollution in Kidsboro is out of control. We are in a crisis situation, and if we do not respond to it right now, we are forfeiting the futures of our children and our children's children."

I could hear Scott chuckling. I dared not look at him. Mark glared in his direction, and Scott buried his head in his hands as if he were crying—mourning the thought of our children's children having lungs like rotten pumpkins. I don't think Mark was fooled, but he continued with his presentation anyway.

It was budget time in Kidsboro, the only town I know of that's completely run by kids. It was May, a year and three months after Kidsboro had first opened its doors, so to speak. Our first budget had been done pretty randomly, so we had decided we needed to be more organized this year and write out a complete budget for the entire year. In Kidsboro, everything was paid for with Kidsboro money—starbills and tokens.

We were meeting to decide what kinds of things the Kidsboro government would pay for with the people's taxes. The first year we'd had only three government employees— Alice, the chief of police, Corey, the garbageman, and me, Ryan Cummings, the mayor. The three of us were paid through taxes. The only other things that were paid for with taxes were city buildings, such as the meeting hall pavilion.

But this year was turning out to be different. People had the idea to try to squeeze as much money as they could out of the government for their own causes. Today we were to hear arguments from groups like Clean Up Kidsboro, trying to convince us to give them money. It was supposed to be a serious time of deciding where our citizens' tax money was going to go, but groups like this made it a circus.

I tried my hardest not to laugh. The people who were representing causes really cared about their issues and expected wise, informed decisions from their government. I cared about the environment too; I just didn't think Kidsboro had a big pollution problem. And that rotten pumpkin was enough to make a dead man giggle.

Despite Scott's stifled laughter, Mark continued straight-faced.

"Listen to this. A poll taken of Kidsboro citizens shows that 85 percent of our population don't want our city to become a scummy pothole of pollution and filth."

Wow. Did that mean 15 percent of our people *did* want our city to become a scummy pothole?

"I think this statistic speaks for itself," he continued. "Kidsboro wants you to do something. Kidsboro *needs* you to do something." He pushed the Stop button on his tape player to put an end to the patriotic background music. He took a deep breath and looked at us like a puppy begging for table scraps.

"What exactly do you want?" I asked him.

Mark picked up some pieces of paper from his notebook and handed them out to each member of the city council.

"On these handouts, I have outlined exactly how much money we'll need for each project that we'll be leading during the upcoming year." We all looked at the paper in front of us. He wanted 30 starbills? That was ridiculous! Very few people made 30 starbills in an entire summer!

"The first project we would like to see approved is the building of an outdoor bathroom. We have noticed some of our citizens—boys—relieving themselves in the creek. This is unacceptable."

An outdoor bathroom was actually not such a bad idea. The nearest building to Kidsboro was Whit's End, the ice cream shop and discovery emporium owned by Mr. Whittaker, or "Whit" as most adults called him. Whit's End was a long way to walk to go to the bathroom in an emergency. But an outdoor bathroom would not cost 30 starbills. And we were all at least nine years old. In my opinion, we could hold it.

"We also need money to increase pollution awareness. Not many people even know there is a problem."

Including me.

Mark continued, "We would also like tougher penalties on littering."

"Is that all?" I asked.

"Yes," he answered.

"All right," I said. "We'll discuss it and get back to you, Mark. Thanks."

"Thank you, Mayor Ryan. Thank you, Scott, Nelson, Alice, Jill," he said, nodding his head toward each council member in turn. "The future of Kidsboro depends on you."

Mark, his two assistants, and his pumpkin left. As soon

as they were out of earshot, Scott's cheeks burst open with laughter, as if he'd been holding his breath for 10 minutes. The rest of us laughed with him.

"I thought I was gonna explode when he brought out the pumpkin!" Scott said.

"Has he been saving that thing since Thanksgiving?" Jill asked.

"What kind of poll was that?" Nelson asked. "How unscientific can you get? You might as well ask a hundred people if they'd like to be eaten by a mountain lion."

The next group approached, and we had to stifle our giggling. But it didn't get any better throughout the rest of the day. More groups came, all so passionate about what they believed in that it almost brought tears to our eyes— especially Scott's eyes, which were about to cry from laughter.

The next group was the farmers, led by Kidsboro's only doctor, James. James had probably joined a special-interest group because he had nothing else to do, since no one trusted him to treat even their slightest wound. I supposed he picked farming because it was the closest thing to medical work, as it dealt with health and nutrition.

The farmers had planted a garden the summer before, but they didn't make any money from it because of a very important premise that they forgot and continued to ignore: Kids don't buy vegetables. In fact, kids usually avoid the vegetable aisle when they go to grocery stores. But the Kidsboro farmers were determined to make us all eat vegetables.

They came to the meeting with charts and graphs showing why it's so important for people to eat healthy foods. I agreed, of course, but I still didn't think kids would *buy* vegetables. The farmers must have had some doubts too, because they wanted the government to subsidize their garden. That meant they wanted the government to buy all of their produce since there was no demand for it from the customers.

Next was Corey, our garbageman, who wanted to be paid as much as Alice and me. We had intended to give him a raise, but he certainly didn't deserve as much as he was asking for. After all, he only worked once a week! And it wasn't as if people were throwing away heavy things like old televisions or charcoal grills. All he had to do was go around collecting candy wrappers, apple cores, soft drink cans, and paper. That was about it. Everything he collected would fit in a small grocery bag.

Next was an animal rights group that wanted dogs and cats to have the same rights in Kidsboro as humans—including citizenship and their own houses. A newer citizen of Kidsboro named Melissa told us a tear-jerking "true" story about a cat that wanted to be an actor in cat food commercials but kept getting thrown off buses. He could never get to Hollywood.

Unless we had some blind citizens or created a fire department, I couldn't fathom what a dog would do for a living in our town. Much less a cat, unless a big hairball fad suddenly swept the city.

The next group was the Legalize Slingshots group, who wanted to put an end to the law in our city charter forbidding slingshots anywhere within the Kidsboro city limits. I thought this was a common-sense law, but the group did their best to shoot holes in it. A boy named Ben stood up and said with all sincerity, "We have a right to protect ourselves against nature. Do you have any idea how many bears there are in this part of the country?" He was right—I didn't have any idea. And I was pretty sure Ben didn't either. The group brought out different kinds of slingshots—some large, some small, some built to fling rocks, some made to fling things like rubber balls. They wanted us to consider each type, noting the ones that were perfectly harmless. But what good would harmless slingshots be against a bear?

Finally, the slingshot guys collected their weapons and displays and headed home. Again, the second they were out of earshot, we all had a big laugh about it. I was still laughing when the next group came up from behind me. Suddenly, everyone else stopped laughing. They looked over my shoulder with faces of stone, not cracking a smile. I turned around.

It was Valerie Swanson, Nelson's sister. She was accompanied by two other girls, and the looks on their faces told us they meant business. Suddenly, things were not so jovial in the meeting hall. Valerie always got what she wanted, and I shivered to think about what she could possibly want now. Everyone else had come to us like desperate souls, worried about the status of the world. Valerie came with a demanding look that said, "I have no concern for you or your city. I just want what I want, and I will get it." Her long, brown hair was pulled back in clips, and I was momentarily distracted by her good looks. I quickly shook it off, knowing that I needed to be at the top of my game to deal with her.

The three girls walked in sync as they approached the

front of the meeting hall. They had no charts, no diagrams, no visual aids—just themselves and whatever frightening cause they were about to stand for.

Valerie, of course, was the spokesperson. "Good afternoon, council members. We represent Girls Against Discrimination." (GAD?) "We have noticed certain inconsistencies with the way our city council, and specifically, our mayor, makes decisions. Our research team has documented evidence that boys are given special privileges in this town. There are more boys than girls in Kidsboro. There are three boys but only two girls on the city council. Boys get better pay. And boys are hired for government jobs before girls. We want these things changed."

There was a short pause. Apparently, this was all she felt she needed to say. She wanted it. Now we were expected to do it. I wouldn't let her get away with this, but I had to act reasonable at the same time. "Valerie," I said calmly, "I've never noticed a pattern of special treatment or consideration given to boys over girls."

"Of course you haven't. You're a boy."

This was her response? I was looking for something more along the lines of this documented evidence she was talking about. "Well . . . Valerie . . ." I continued, sounding a bit too much like I was talking to a three year old, "you've got to have more solid evidence than vague accusations. You need to make an argument."

"Oh, I will. Just not here."

"Then where?"

Valerie reached into her back pocket and pulled out a

folded sheet of paper. She handed it to me. I unfolded it, and across the top of the page was the word *Subpoena*, which meant she was taking me to court. "I'm suing you," she said.

"For what?"

"Discrimination."

I looked around at the rest of the city council, trying to feel their support. But all I got were looks that said, "You're on your own, buddy."

I stiffened my upper lip. "Is this supposed to scare me into giving you whatever you want?"

"Oh, I'll get what I want."

"And what's that?"

"More government jobs for girls. Another girl on the city council. Equal pay for equal work. And no more new boys will come in as citizens until there are just as many girls here as there are boys."

I chuckled and hoped the rest of the city council would follow my lead and chuckle with me. They didn't. "Valerie . . . you know, I would love to . . . but there's not much I can do about—"

"See you in court," she said, gesturing to the other girls to follow her out. They were gone before I could get another word out.

I looked at the other council members. I started laughing again, just like I had laughed at all the others. "Does she really think that . . . Ha! She's so . . . silly . . . " I scanned their faces, but no one was laughing with me this time.

Jill stared at me with a scrunched up nose. "Why *are* there three boys but only two girls on the city council?"

I gulped hard.

Alice glanced at me with the same look. "How much money do you and Corey make?"

● ● ●

I wasn't paying much attention to what Mr. Whittaker and Nelson were working on, but whatever it was, I knew it would be amazing when it was done. It was things like this that made Whit's End more than just an ice cream place. Mr. Whittaker was a great inventor who taught all the kids who came into his shop about the Bible (and life in general) through his machines. He and Nelson were working on the Imagination Station, which was sort of like a time machine that let you live in other times. At the moment, they were working on a Bible program for the story of Joshua.

"Could you read off those numbers, Nelson?" Mr. Whittaker asked.

"Sure."

"Thanks."

Nelson read off a list of numbers from a sheet of paper. The list made no sense to me, but Mr. Whittaker pounded them all into the keyboard.

I waited for Nelson to finish, and then asked the question that had been dominating my thoughts ever since Valerie and her friends had made their announcement. "Do you think I discriminate against girls?"

Nelson took off his glasses and put one earpiece in his mouth. He looked thoughtful for a few moments, and then said without a doubt, "No." He looked back at the computer screen, where Mr. Whittaker's program was loading.

"That's it? No explanation?"

"My response doesn't require an explanation. If I had answered 'Yes, I do think you discriminate,' then it would require an explanation. But I said no." He was beginning to sound more and more like Eugene Meltsner, Odyssey's resident genius and Nelson's mentor.

"May I ask why you're asking that question, Ryan?" Mr. Whittaker asked. I told him about Valerie's new feminist group.

"I've never known you to make any decisions that discriminated against girls," Mr. Whittaker said.

"Yeah," Nelson said, "you're always suggesting girls when we vote on new citizens."

"And you seem to get along with most of them," Mr. Whittaker added.

"Yeah," I said, my head raised a little higher. "I *do* get along with girls. I don't discriminate. I'm very fair. Right?"

"Right," Nelson said, his attention back on the computer.

"I don't have to just sit here and accept what Valerie says. I've got plenty of evidence on my side. I can beat her in court!"

"Sure you can."

"I need to write some stuff down," I said, but before I could find any paper, Scott walked up.

"Hey, did you meet the guy from the *Odyssey Times*?" he asked excitedly.

"No."

"He came out to Kidsboro today and asked me a bunch of questions."

"About what?"

"The town, how it worked . . . he asked a lot of questions about you."

"Really?"

"Wouldn't that be cool if there was an article in the paper about Kidsboro?"

"That would be great," Mr. Whittaker said.

"Hey, he'll probably want to interview both of you," Scott said, referring to Mr. Whittaker and me.

"Yeah, that's right, Mr. Whittaker," I said. "He'll want to know how the place started." Having a town run by kids had been Mr. Whittaker's idea. He'd founded Kidsboro and had helped us build the town.

I coached Mr. Whittaker on some of the things to talk about when the *Odyssey Times* reporter came to him. Mr. Whittaker chuckled, knowing exactly what to say. He always did.

TWO

JUSTICE IS SERVED

ALL COURT CASES TOOK place in the meeting hall pavilion, the same place where the city council met. Kidsboro had 36 citizens now, and it seemed like every one of them was there. There were people crammed in under the roof, plus there were more than a dozen outside looking in. A few outsiders were also there either because they were interested in our justice system, or they were just bored. The chance to see somebody get sued always seemed to draw a crowd, but this was an even bigger event. The mayor was getting sued.

Because no crime had been committed, this was considered a civil case. Civil cases that required an interpretation of the law were not heard before a jury, only a judge. Judge Amy came out in the long, black robe that her brother had used for his high-school graduation. She looked very official but a little intimidating. Still, I wasn't worried by the fact that this was a "boy versus girl" case and Amy was a girl. She had always been fair. In matters of justice, I didn't trust anyone as much as I trusted Judge Amy.

Valerie was wearing a business suit and had her hair up in

a bun on top of her head. I knew her strategy. She wanted to look as much like a boy as possible, so that people would begin to see fewer differences between girls and boys. She wanted everyone to know that the two were equal. This was one of the few times in Kidsboro history that anyone had worn a suit within its city limits. I wore jeans with a hole in the knee.

Valerie winked at me when she sat down at the opposite table. I hated it when girls flirted with me and didn't mean it.

Judge Amy called the place to attention with her gavel. Everyone fell silent. "All right, state your cases," she said. "Valerie, you go first."

Valerie stood up. If there had been a jury at this point, she would've smiled at them and flung her hair back. Of course, every boy on the jury would have immediately been on her side when she did that. But since there was only Amy to impress, her face remained rock-hard and serious. "Your Honor, I'm here to state my case against Ryan Cummings, who I believe has discriminated against girls during his tenure as mayor here in Kidsboro. I have documented evidence that proves he has given special privileges to boys."

"Documented evidence?" Amy asked.

"Yes. May I approach the bench, Your Honor?" I knew this won her big points with the judge—asking permission to approach the bench. Wow.

"Yes."

Valerie walked up to where Amy was sitting and held out a cassette tape and a stack of papers for her to see. Then she turned and spoke loudly so that the crowd could hear. "In these documents, I have statistics that prove an obvious imbalance in Mayor Ryan's nominations for citizens of Kidsboro, as well as how he hands out government jobs. As you can see here, there are 36 citizens of Kidsboro, and 23 of them are boys—or 63 percent. The government has developed a number of city projects in which it hired workers for a couple of weeks at a time. They hired 27 workers for all of these projects. Twenty-two of them were boys." There was some murmuring from the crowd. But she wasn't done.

"On average, boys make eight starbills a month more than girls in Kidsboro." More murmuring, and this time I noticed that most of it was female murmurs. I didn't want to turn around in case every girl in the place was staring at me. Valerie went on. "And, of course, I find it very convenient that there are three boys on the city council but only two girls. Mayor Cummings is obviously anti-girl."

Valerie glanced at me with a smirk on her face and reached behind her chair. She pulled out a tape player. "Let me show you just how anti-girl he is."

What did she have on that tape?

"On this tape, I have the voice of Ryan Cummings, our mayor. I'm sure you'll recognize it immediately. You will hear Ryan share his true feelings about girls. This is a taped interview that Ryan did with the *Kidsboro Chronicle* last winter when Jill did an article on the Kidsboro military. Listen carefully, if you will." I shot a look at Jill, who had her head down. She refused to make eye contact.

Valerie pressed Play, and out came Jill's voice. "Ryan, there are many girls who have volunteered to be in our army. What do you think their role will be?"

The next voice was mine. "Oh, the girls will play a vital role in our military. They'll be right there when the fighting starts . . . serving the guys hot chocolate."

Valerie quickly pressed Stop and looked out at the audience. I was too shocked to look around, but I could feel the red-hot stares of all the girls, plus the utter disbelief of all the boys.

I had only been making a joke, and Jill knew that.

Valerie continued. "A person who thinks this way about girls can't make decisions without his bias getting in the way. And indeed, I believe it *does* get in the way. Ryan runs a city where girls are in the minority, where girls make less money, and where boys get more and better jobs in the government. I cannot just sit back and watch this happen to my gender."

There was some female applause from the back. I glanced over, and Scott was doing sort of a half-clap, which meant that he didn't exactly agree with Valerie, but he also didn't want to get attacked by a bunch of angry girls afterward either.

I had to admit that Valerie was well prepared. I'd had no idea she was going to have statistics and a tape, and for a few moments, I wondered if I really was a girl hater. But I had to go ahead and state my case. I knew in my heart that I wasn't a girl hater, and I had to prove it.

"Is that all?" Amy asked Valerie.

"Yes."

"All right. Your turn, Ryan."

I stood up and tucked my shirt into my pants. Nothing I could do would make me look as professional as Valerie, but I also didn't want to be a slob. Sloppiness might somehow make me look like a girl-hating man.

"I would like to answer all these claims, Your Honor. May I approach the bench?"

"Yes."

I approached, but then I realized I had nothing to give to her and no reason to approach the bench. I just wanted to extend to her the same respect that Valerie had. I got up there and immediately took a couple of steps back. "First, I'd like to talk about this '63 percent of all Kidsborians are boys' thing. Now, if you ask anyone on the city council, I am always suggesting girls as new citizens. But for some reason, girls are less likely to want to join our town than boys. Maybe they think that clubhouses are boy kinds of things."

I sensed some seething behind me, like I had just offended somebody, but I went on. "In fact, in the history of Kidsboro, only six boys have turned down our offers to become citizens, while 13 girls have declined to become citizens. I have the city council records . . ." I whirled around and realized I hadn't planned as well as I thought I had. "I have them on my computer at home. I'll get you a copy. Second, I want to talk about the government projects Valerie mentioned. Let me list those projects: rebuilding the bridge this spring, paving the roads in the middle of town last summer, moving those huge rocks on the edge of town so that we could create a sports field—all of these projects required hard, manual labor that girls are not built for." I heard hissing from the back.

"I'm sorry, but except for Alice, I don't think there are any girls in here who could've moved those rocks." Male clapping and female hissing.

"Order," Amy called out.

"As for the salaries, how can Valerie bring up salaries? This town has business owners and independent workers. Their salaries are based on how much they sell and how much work they do. The government has nothing to do with the salaries of anyone but Alice, Corey, and me. And Alice makes more than Corey. I don't doubt that boys make more money—just look at Nelson, for example. Nelson's inventions always sell like hotcakes. He's very rich. He raises the average all by himself. Of course the boys' average is gonna be more. Nelson makes as much as 10 boys!"

The boys' applause drowned out the girls' hissing.

"Valerie's statistics are misleading. I believe that I have made very fair decisions in my time here, and I will continue to do so. As for that tape . . . I was clearly making a joke! If Valerie had let that tape play just a few seconds longer, I'm sure I said the words 'just kidding' and laughed or something. I don't feel that way at all about girls. Just look at my record." I sat down to some mild applause.

"Okay. Thank you, Ryan." Judge Amy's face wrinkled up, and she tapped her gavel on the table several times. "All right," she said, "I'd like to listen to the entire tape."

Valerie stood up in instant protest. "Why, Your Honor?"

"I want to hear context. I want to hear what Ryan said right after he made the comment about girls."

"Your Honor, with all due respect, the context makes no difference. The fact is he said it, whether he was joking or not."

"I'll make that call, not you," she said. I liked Judge Amy.

Valerie breathed a heavy breath of protest, and then retrieved her tape player.

"Rewind back to the beginning of Jill's question," Amy said.

Valerie obeyed. The tape came on in the middle of Jill's question.

". . . girls who have volunteered to be in our army. What do you think their role will be?"

"Oh, the girls will play a vital role in our military. They'll be right there when the fighting starts . . . serving the guys hot chocolate." I laughed. "Just kidding. You're not gonna print that, are you?" Valerie stopped the tape.

"Wait," Amy said. "Let it go. I want to hear how he really answered the question." Valerie let out another breath of protest and pressed Play. I loved Judge Amy.

I continued. "I don't really see any different roles for girls. They're just as capable as boys are of doing the things that army training calls for."

"Okay, stop the tape," Amy said. Valerie rolled her eyes. She stopped the tape but didn't sit down.

"Your Honor, this was a newspaper interview. He was just saying what he thought the readers wanted him to say. His true feelings are the things that remain unpublished."

"That's not for you to say, Valerie. Now, I'm going to leave for a few minutes and make my decision. Court is in recess." She banged her gavel.

I believed I was out of trouble. But one thing really bothered me. Why did Jill give her that tape?

I turned around to look at her, but she was no longer there. I whirled around and saw her practically running toward her clubhouse. I went after her.

"Jill!" I shouted before she made it inside her office. She stopped suddenly, but she didn't turn around.

I had to walk around her to get her attention, because she stubbornly refused to turn around. I looked straight at her. "Why did you give Valerie that tape?"

"I remembered that joke."

"You knew I was joking."

"Maybe I didn't think it was that funny."

"You know me, Jill. You know I don't hate girls."

"Maybe not. But I'm starting to see what Valerie is talking about."

"What?"

"Government jobs usually do go to boys. You definitely suggest boys for citizenship more often than girls."

"Are you actually joining Valerie's GAD group?"

"No, of course not. I know better than to follow Valerie. But I'm just trying to make sure our world doesn't work like the real world."

"What do you mean?"

"Women are sometimes discriminated against. There are women who get paid less for doing the same jobs men do. I think Kidsboro should be different."

I fumed. "Did you think of that yourself, or did Valerie come up with that?"

She fumed right back. "Believe it or not, Ryan, girls can think for themselves. Even me." She stormed off back toward the meeting hall; obviously, she didn't really need to go to her office. I followed 30 steps behind her.

Judge Amy sat down in her seat. The crowd was as quiet as 40 adolescents and preadolescents could get. She folded her hands and peered out over the audience.

"Mayor Cummings," she began, fixing her gaze on me, "your joke wasn't funny. Boys are not smarter than girls, and girls are not less capable than boys. Whether you were joking or not, the attitude that girls are not as valuable as boys are should be avoided at all times. You should know better, being in the public eye. If I were you, I would watch what I say, on and off the record."

She stopped looking at me and directed her attention to the audience again. "But I do believe it was a joke. I don't believe that this joke is evidence that Ryan truly feels that way. I also don't believe that any of the other evidence Valerie presented shows he feels that way either."

She turned toward Valerie, who had her arms crossed and her teeth clinched. "Valerie, you presented a strong case, but I must rule in favor of the mayor. Court's adjourned."

She banged the gavel, and the whole place erupted with opinions. A number of the girls were livid, and some of the boys were relieved. I heard the word "appeal" come from Valerie's lips, but Kidsboro had no court for her to appeal to. We only had one court, and it had just ruled in my favor. Whether or not she had a court to appeal to, though, I knew very well that Valerie was not through with me.

Jill was gone the second Amy's gavel hit the table.

• • •

There aren't very many people who get the best of Valerie Swanson. So as I strolled into Kidsboro the next morning, I held my head a little higher than normal. I probably walked a little more quickly, my feet a little lighter. I greeted everyone I saw. "Hi, Marcy. Hey, Mark. Hi, Pete. How's it goin', Sid?"

But there was something strange going on. No one was saying hi back. They all just stared at me, like I had an extra nose this morning. My inner joy turned to inner confusion as I was a one-man parade through a crowd of people turning to each other and whispering. No one spoke to me, but everyone seemed to be speaking *about* me.

What was going on?

I asked this question of a few of the gawkers, but no one would answer. I guess no one wanted to be the one to tell me what was so terribly wrong.

I ducked into my office, eager to be out of the spotlight. Scott was at my desk, reading a newspaper.

"Why is everybody acting so weird?" I asked.

Scott looked at me in shock. "Is any of this true?" he said.

"Is any of what true?"

He slid the paper across the table. It was the *Barnacle*, the weekly newspaper printed in Bettertown, the rival town across the creek. The *Barnacle* always made fun of the *Kidsboro Chronicle* and everything about Kidsboro.

On the front page, in big bold letters, were the words: "Kidsboro Mayor Has Secret Past."

I started sweating.

THREE

THE SECRET REVEALED

THERE IT WAS FOR everyone to see—my secret past. And whoever had written the article hadn't missed many details.

KIDSBORO MAYOR HAS SECRET PAST

Kidsboro—Ryan Cummings, mayor of Kidsboro, is not who he appears to be. According to a source who wishes to remain anonymous, Ryan Cummings is actually Jim Bowers, a former resident of the San Francisco area. He and his mother ran from California and changed their names for "personal reasons." Also, in direct contrast to the mayor's claims over the last five years is the resurrection of his father, who Ryan (or is that Jim?) said was dead. The source explained that Ryan's father is very much alive.

The article went on about some other lies I'd told. There was a picture of me from my third-grade yearbook. The caption read "Jim Bowers." I hadn't changed much since the third grade. That was me, all right. The truth was that my mom and I had left California to escape my abusive, alcoholic father.

My second biggest fear—after my dad finding my mom and me—had always been that my friends would find out who I really was. And here it was, in black and white. Scott saw that I was done reading the article. "What's this all about?" he asked.

I looked at him, but couldn't answer. I crumpled up the paper, threw it down, and ran out of my office.

Jill was right outside the door. I switched directions to get past her, but she stuck her arm out. "Ryan, what's going on?" I didn't want to talk to her, even though I knew she probably wouldn't put anything I said in the paper. I kept going.

I heard footsteps running up behind me, and I glanced back. It was Valerie. She had the biggest smile on her face. I sped up, but not before she got some verbal shots in. "Hey, Ryan," she said, "you remember in our election last year, how you told everyone that you had never lied to them? I was just wondering: Does that include the time when you lied about everything?"

Done digging in her heels, she slowed down and let me go. Dozens of people were watching. I didn't know where I was running. I was just furious with everyone and everything right now.

But then something dawned on me. I stopped and addressed the onlookers. "Has anyone seen Jake?"

Jake Randall was the one who had told my story. I just knew it. He'd been a neighbor of mine in California before we had moved. He'd visited his grandmother in Odyssey last summer and had a stranglehold on me because of what he knew about my past. I believed he had just returned to Odyssey for summer vacation. I was going after him.

Someone in the crowd answered my question. "I just saw Jake at Whit's End about 20 minutes ago," he said. I was gone before he could finish his sentence.

● ● ●

Whit's End was crowded when I burst through the door, but I barely even noticed. Jake was standing in a corner of the shop, next to a tall indoor plant. I went straight for him. He saw me coming and must have known why I was there, because he stopped talking to Max.

"You just couldn't keep your fat mouth shut, could you?" I said.

"I didn't tell him nothing, man."

"Liar!"

"You've got the wrong guy, dude," he said with a smirk. I hated that look, and somehow it sparked an uncontrollable anger in me. I wasn't going to look at that face anymore. Suddenly, my fist clenched up and I let it fly. I hit him square in the jaw. He was caught off-balance and fell backward into the plant. The sides of the pot broke apart underneath him, sending dirt in all directions. The crowd fell silent as I looked at him. That wasn't me that had just punched someone. I didn't hit people. Jake looked up at me with blood streaming from his chin, more shocked than hurt.

Mr. Whittaker ran up just as Jake got to his feet and charged at me. Mr. Whittaker grabbed Jake by the chest, and his punch missed me by a foot. Mr. Whittaker forced him to the wall.

"What's going on?" Mr. Whittaker asked.

Max spoke up with shocked glee. "Ryan clocked him."

"What?"

"Right in the jaw."

Mr. Whittaker looked at me in disbelief, and then he looked at Jake. "Are you okay?"

"Yeah. Just caught me off guard," he said, loosening up to show that he wasn't going to charge me again. He pointed at me. "If that punch woulda hurt, you'd be lyin' in a ditch sometime tomorrow."

"That's enough, Jake," said Mr. Whittaker.

"I never said a word to that reporter," Jake continued.

"Let me see your face," Mr. Whittaker insisted. Jake moved his hand and Mr. Whittaker looked it over. "I don't think it needs stitches. You want a ride home?"

Jake shook his head. "I'm okay."

Mr. Whittaker turned his attention to me. His face was rock-hard. "I *am* taking *you* home, Ryan."

● ● ●

"You want to tell me what that was all about?" Mr. Whittaker asked in his car on the way to my house. I had seen him angry before, but never at me.

"I don't feel like talking about it," I said, not looking at him. I didn't want to hear any advice. I wanted to be mad for a while. I didn't want him to make me regret hitting Jake. I knew I would probably feel bad about it later, but right now

I was enjoying the memory of his bloody chin. He was trying to ruin my life. I was glad I had at least ruined his chin for a moment.

Mr. Whittaker must have known what I was thinking, because he allowed me to keep my feelings to myself. He probably knew that I would tell him everything in time.

My mother wasn't quite as understanding. The second Mr. Whittaker and I walked through the door, she wanted to know exactly what had happened.

"You hit him?" she exclaimed.

"I'm sorry." It was all I could say.

"Why did you do it?"

I glanced at Mr. Whittaker, who I knew was anxious to hear my explanation. "You don't have to say why in front of me, Ryan," he said.

"No, you can stay," I replied. I looked at my mother, whose face had an odd expression—somewhere between fury and sympathy—knowing something heavy was going to come out of my mouth. "Jake told a reporter all about us. It's in the Bettertown newspaper. Everyone knows everything."

My mom put her hand over her mouth, and her fury instantly vanished. "Everything?"

"Except for Dad. He wasn't mentioned, except to say that he's alive."

"I should call Mr. Henson." Mr. Henson was the agent assigned to keep us safe. We knew my dad was close by, because he had called our house the previous winter. He knew what state we were in but possibly nothing more. He could narrow it down to an area code, but our next three digits didn't give away anything. The local exchange numbers Mr. Henson had given to us weren't found anywhere else in the state. But the more word got out about us, the easier it would be for him to find us.

● ● ●

Mr. Henson came by to talk to all of us. My mother asked Mr. Whittaker to stay for emotional support, and he did.

"We'll confiscate all copies of the newspaper," he said.

"There's a reporter for the *Odyssey Times* that's been asking questions in Kidsboro," I said. "What if the *Times* gets it?"

"I can talk to Dale Jacobs," Mr. Whittaker said. Dale Jacobs was the editor. "I'll make sure he doesn't print this."

"Good," Mr. Henson said. He sighed and looked at my mom and me. "Listen, I want to give you this option one more time. I know you like Odyssey, but we can safely move you away. We can change your names again, change everything."

I loved Odyssey, and I never wanted to move. Mom and I exchanged pitiful looks. I was sure she was feeling the same way I was. "I'm tired of running, Mr. Henson," she told him. "This is the place I want to be. I'm not going to let him dictate our lives anymore."

"Ms. Cummings," Mr. Henson said, looking to Mr. Whittaker to see if he would back him up, "this is for your own safety."

"I know it is, and I appreciate your concern. But we need to put an end to this now. If he finds us once, he'll find us again."

Mr. Henson breathed heavily and stood up from the couch. "I'll put the police on alert. We have his picture up at the station. Everybody knows who to look for. But if you change your mind . . ." He looked at my mom and must have decided not to finish his sentence. She would not change her mind.

He glanced at me before he went out the door. "The article didn't mention the abuse. Don't tell your friends about it. The more you tell, the more danger you put them in if he comes around asking questions." He nodded to Mr. Whittaker and left.

● ● ●

There was no pretending it never happened. Everywhere I went I was reminded that I was no longer Ryan, mayor of Kidsboro. I was now Jim, the fraud who punches people. I tried to slink to my office unnoticed, but all my friends wanted to know if the *Barnacle* story was true, and all my enemies wanted to dig their nails into my skin.

The last person I wanted to see, Max, ran over from Bettertown to see me. "Jimbo! Hey, buddy!"

"Go away, Max."

"Wow. It's true. You really are a new man. I like it. You're not gonna punch me, are you? You know, I'm definitely voting for you in the next election."

"You don't get a vote."

"Oh, I'll get my vote in there somehow."

"I've got stuff to do."

"Oh, that's right. Mayor stuff. Bills to sign, laws to write, people to send to the hospital . . ."

"Go back to your own town."

"You know, you've inspired me. I'm thinking about completely changing my image too. Hey, you'd know this. Where would I go for a fake ID card?"

"Max—"

"No, just call me Dirk from now on. I think I look more like a Dirk."

"I have a meeting."

"It must be so cool to be able to reinvent yourself like that. Nobody even knows who you are anymore. Not even your friends. The only thing we all know for sure is that you're a liar and a thug."

I had tried my best to ignore him, but his last statement struck me. Did my *friends* really feel this way?

● ● ●

We held a scheduled city council meeting to discuss the new budget, but when I got to the meeting hall, the only item on anyone's agenda was getting to the bottom of the whole Jim Bowers story.

I sat down and took out my notes. No one was there to discuss the budget. They all just stared at me like I didn't belong anymore. I needed to get this over with.

"It's all true," I said. "I lied about my past because I had to. I can't really tell you any more than that. It's about my family, and it's very personal, and I hope you can understand that I . . . I just can't talk about it. I was upset that the information got out, and that's why I hit Jake. I shouldn't have done it, but I did. I'll apologize as soon as I see him. Could we please not mention it again?"

I could tell from their faces that they were not satisfied with my answer. They probably felt betrayed because I didn't trust them, but apparently nobody trusted *me*, either.

No one said anything for a solid minute. I stared at my hands. My city council sat there frustrated, not allowed to ask any of the hundred questions that must have been on their lips.

Finally, Scott asked a pretty harmless one. "Do you want us to call you Jim?"

"No," I said firmly. "I'm Ryan."

After another few quiet moments, Police Chief Alice spoke up. "Mayor, I must ask you this. Are you and your mother fugitives from the law?"

"No," I said, even more firmly. "Absolutely not."

"I had to ask," she said. I rolled my eyes.

Then Jill said, "Ryan, look . . . I know you have to keep this whole thing secret, but I'm afraid you're going to have to say *something*."

"Why, so you can get a juicy story?" I said, more harshly than I probably should have.

"You have an image problem, Ryan. Nobody trusts you anymore."

"What do you mean?"

"I did a poll for tomorrow's edition of the *Chronicle*. Your approval numbers are way down. From 78 percent to 33 percent. You lied to everybody, Ryan."

"Well, what was I supposed to do?"

"I don't know, but you need to fix it."

"It would be nice if I had some help from the press. It would be nice if the press didn't print that my approval numbers are down to 33 percent. Maybe if my closest friends didn't think I was a fugitive from the law, I could convince other people to trust me. You think that might make it easier?"

I threw my papers down, and they scattered across the floor. Without looking at any of them, I stomped off and left Kidsboro.

FOUR

KISSING AND MAKING UP

I THREW OPEN THE door to my room and slammed my note-book on the desk. I could stay in my room for the summer. I didn't have to go back to Kidsboro. Maybe Mr. Henson was right. Maybe we could leave Odyssey and just start over again. I could make new friends—ones who would trust me. I could start a new Kidsboro in . . . I don't know, Florida or someplace. Maybe I could be this new kid in Florida like Max was talking about. One that hits people. I hadn't had much luck lately being the nice, fair, leader type.

I laid down on my bed with my arms crossed, ready to give up on everything. I wanted to lay here until all this was over.

I gazed around. My room was littered with Kidsboro stuff. On my wall was the Kidsboro flag, which looked just like the American flag, only with thinner stripes and a tree in the field of blue instead of stars. There was a framed copy of the *Kidsboro Chronicle* in which Jill had interviewed me, the brand new mayor, just a year before. The city charter was bound and sitting on my bookshelf. I'd helped write it, and I was very proud of what we had written.

My desk had folders of paperwork scattered across it. I got up and was about to throw it all away when something caught my eye. The proposal from Valerie's feminist group lay on top. The farmers' budget was underneath it, followed by the Clean Up Kidsboro plan to save the Earth.

I shouldn't have laughed at them. They all had concerns and needs and looked to their government to help them. There was nothing wrong with that. If I had been a true leader, I would've compromised. I would've found a way to make their plans work.

Perhaps I wasn't a good leader at all. Maybe that was the real problem. Maybe I couldn't be trusted because there was nothing in me that was worthy of trust.

I sat down at my desk and began leafing through all the proposals. For some reason, I suddenly didn't see anything so unreasonable in these requests. These people had probably worked just as hard on their proposals as I had worked putting together the city charter. Was it right for me to just shoot them down?

I grabbed a pencil and my notebook with new energy and started writing furiously. I could make this work. They would all see that I hadn't lost my ability to lead. A 33 percent approval rating indeed! I would double that number by the weekend.

● ● ●

People were still whispering about me as I passed them on the way into Kidsboro the next day, but I didn't care. I had five copies of my 10-page proposal under my arm and I was ready to present it to the city council. I had worked on it until 11:30 the night before. It was well thought out, organized, and in my eyes, un-rejectable.

I was the first one in the meeting hall, but the other four members filed in just after me.

"You're here?" Scott asked, as if he expected my hasty exit from the last meeting to have been my last.

"Yep," I said with a smile.

"You're happy?"

"Yep."

Everyone arrived with pretty much the same response. They were all unsure, even hesitant to sit down. Was this the same person who'd stomped out of the city council meeting just the day before?

I got right to it. "I wrote a budget plan last night. I reconsidered the proposals given to us by all of the groups that made their presentations the other day, and I think I've come up with some good compromises."

"Compromises?" Nelson asked as he took a proposal and handed another to Jill.

"Yes. I think we were too quick to turn these people away. Some of the things they asked for were quite reasonable—"

"Which ones?" Nelson asked.

"You can read it all right there. I haven't given in to every demand, just the ones that make sense."

They all looked at the plan with their mouths wide open.

"You're giving money to Clean Up Kidsboro?" Jill asked.

"Not as much as they wanted, but yes. We should care about the environment. And I think the outdoor bathroom was a good idea."

"You want to legalize slingshots?" Alice asked, probably because she had never been allowed to carry a weapon herself, yet other people were going to get to.

"On a limited basis: only the small slingshots and not within the city limits. Only in designated slingshot areas."

"Wow. You're giving the feminists everything?" Jill asked.

"Not everything. I think we should agree to give girls more government jobs. And we'll look into equal salaries for boys and girls. I'm still against adding another girl to the city council because that would make six people, which will create a lot of ties. But I'm open to the possibility."

Alice turned to the feminist page and her eyes widened. She apparently liked what she saw.

It was Scott's turn. "You're doubling Corey's salary? He's a garbageman! He's making more than me!" This was a weak comparison since Scott barely made any money from his detective agency.

"He has to pick up garbage. It's disgusting, and he should be paid well for it. I'm not giving him what he asked for, only part."

They continued to read through the proposal, glued to every word. Their heads nodded, except for Nelson's. "We can't do this," he said. "This is going to cost too much. We don't have this kind of money."

"That's not for us to decide. That's for the taxpayers to

decide. They're the ones who are going to be paying for all of it."

"Taxes are going to go through the roof."

"It'll be a sacrifice."

"It'll be a suicide. They'll be paying half their salaries in taxes," Nelson said.

"When we bring this proposal before the town, we'll explain all of that. It's up to them," I insisted.

"We can't bring this before the town."

"That's what we're here to vote on. The city council votes on what we present to the town. If you don't like it, don't vote for it."

"This is insane!" Nelson said loudly.

"That's fine if you think that, but the rest of us might not agree with you. Has everybody had a chance to read it?" I asked.

They all nodded.

"Okay, then I say we vote on it. Who votes that we present this budget plan to the town? Raise your hands."

I raised my hand immediately. Alice, Jill, and Scott leafed through the plan, skimming the main points before they made their decision. Nelson had his hands on his hips, amazed that we were even considering this. Scott flipped over the last page and raised his hand. I knew his reasoning. He didn't care about high taxes because he made so little money that it wouldn't affect him that much. He was probably excited about using a slingshot.

Jill breathed a heavy sigh and raised her hand. She was

probably pleased that I was giving in to the feminist group and would vote for it based solely on that.

Alice liked the part about equal salaries for girls. The Clean Up Kidsboro section mentioned harsher penalties for litterers. I'm sure the vision of throwing litterers to the ground and handcuffing them flashed before her eyes. She lived for moments like that. She raised her hand without hesitation.

Nelson bowed his head in his hand. "This is a mistake," he said.

"The town doesn't have to vote for it."

"Can I campaign against it?" he asked.

"Go right ahead," I said, even though I didn't like the idea of the town seeing that the city council was divided.

● ● ●

Jill printed a special edition of the *Kidsboro Chronicle*, which included the entire budget in chart form and a written explanation of what each of the items in the chart meant. Jill also wrote up a point/counterpoint-type article in which she interviewed both Nelson and me to show the opposing sides to the issue. Nelson's essay on tax increases and government waste was well written, scary, and probably very effective. I wrote my essay on the government's responsibility to take care of its citizens and the citizens' responsibility to take care of each other. Both gave the reader something to think about, which was the point. The article ended by informing everyone that we would vote on the budget in a citywide vote the next day at four o'clock at the meeting hall.

One very nice thing happened after this article came out. People started looking me in the eye again, especially people who were members of the groups that would benefit from this budget. Mark, head of Clean Up Kidsboro, smiled at me as I walked past him. The farmers were reading the article as I passed them, and they gave me a thumbs-up sign. Even Valerie gave me a slight grin.

Suddenly, I felt like the mayor again. I had made them forget about Jim Bowers.

● ● ●

I would stack Kidsboro's voting record against that of any country. In the United States, only about 50 percent of registered voters vote. But in Kidsboro, everybody votes. I like to think it's because we care about the issues that affect our city and our lives. But if I wanted to be honest about it, it's probably because we have such a small number of citizens. Everyone knows exactly how important his or her vote is.

Maybe people must have thought that this vote was going to be close, because everyone showed up at the ballot box the next day. The meeting hall was packed. I looked around at all the people and tried to figure it out. Valerie's group, plus the Clean Up Kidsboro group, plus the farmers, plus the slingshotters, plus the animal rights guys . . . It appeared that there were about 16 or so people in the hall who were in at least one of these groups. If I had all of their votes, I would need only a few more people to agree to the budget for it to pass.

There was a big box on the front table with a hole in the

top. Everyone waited for the polls to open. We'd agreed that there would be a brief discussion time before we started.

Jill was the moderator. She stood up and called for attention. "Does anyone have anything they want to say before we start the voting?"

Nelson popped up immediately. "This budget plan would send taxes soaring. The economy wouldn't be able to handle it."

A boy stood up in the back. "He's right. And what are we spending our money on? We don't need slingshots and bathrooms. We especially don't need vegetables."

Nelson raised his hand. "I have a suggestion. Can we at least vote on all these items separately? One vote for the slingshots, another for the farmers . . ."

Mark stood up and addressed Nelson directly. "No! Then everybody would just vote for their own cause, and nothing would get passed. It's all or nothing."

"This budget could bankrupt us," Nelson stated.

"The only reason you care so much is that you're rich. You'll have to pay the most in taxes," Mark said.

Everybody started speaking at once, and none of it was audible. Mark was right. Nelson was the richest person in town, and if we took a percentage of income from each person in Kidsboro, the rich would have to pay a lot more than anyone else.

Jill yelled at the top of her lungs, but couldn't restore order. After a few moments of utter mayhem, she stood up on the table. "Quiet!!!"

The noise subsided. She cleared her throat. "Does anyone

have anything constructive to say?" I raised my hand. "Yes, Ryan?" She nodded at me.

I stood up and turned to face as many people as I could. "I understand how Nelson feels. But I think we should always be looking for ways to make this city better. The only way we can do that is through the sacrifices of our people. It will be a sacrifice for us, yes. No doubt about it, taxes will increase, but the rewards could be great." This was followed by the applause of about half of those present.

"Why do we need more girls in this town?" an unidentified boy shouted from the back. "We've got too many as it is!"

If this kid had set off a bomb, it would've caused less of a stir. There wasn't a closed mouth in the whole place. Girls were yelling at boys, boys were yelling at girls, farmers were yelling at meat-eaters, environmentalists were yelling at big-business polluters. It took Jill a full five minutes to calm everyone down.

"Okay, no more discussion! We're just gonna vote on this thing! Form a single-file line at the box. Alice will give you a piece of paper. Write down your vote and put it into the box."

The process was remarkably civilized, considering that everyone had been at each other's throats just moments before. Everybody cast his or her vote, and then the polls closed. Jill and Alice voted last, and then they took the box to be counted. It didn't take long to count 36 votes, so I knew we would get the results almost immediately.

Alice and Jill came back with a piece of paper. Alice held it in her hand as she stood at the table. The crowd was motionless as she unfolded the paper. Not one for dramatics,

Alice came right out with it. "The budget passes, 20 to 16."

The place erupted with simultaneous joy and pain. Nelson buried his head in his hands. Valerie's feminists jumped up and down and hugged. The farmers pulled metal trowels out of their pockets and started waving them back and forth. The animal rights group barked like dogs.

Nelson looked up long enough to make eye contact with me. He shook his head and left.

● ● ●

The new laws went into effect immediately. My first order of business was to deal with Valerie and the feminists, because I knew they would make a big fuss over getting what they wanted before anybody else did. I thought about government jobs, and the one that came to mind as I stared out at my big list of things to do was to get myself a secretary. Of course, I would have to call her an "administrative assistant" to please the feminists. An assistant would take a lot of the burden off of me.

I looked over my list of citizens, and one name stood out: Lauren Luzinski. She had never held a steady job, so she was definitely available to work. She had never done anything to catch my attention in either a good way or a bad way, so perhaps this would be a chance for her to stand out for once. She could sit in on city council meetings and take notes.

I informed Valerie that I was going to hire Lauren, and she was pleased. Lauren had not been a member of Valerie's feminist group, but she was a girl and that was enough.

Lauren was surprised when I asked her. "You want me to be your administrative assistant?"

"Yep."

"Why?"

"Because . . . I think you'd do a good job."

"Really?" she said, her eyes sparkling.

"Sure. You interested?"

"Well . . . yeah. I'd love to."

"Then you're hired."

"Wow." I felt like I had just told her she'd won the lottery.

"Come on, then. I'll show you everything."

● ● ●

"I believe a new day has dawned in Kidsboro. We are now not just—"

"Too fast."

"Oh. Sorry." I was dictating a press release to Lauren. She was writing down everything that came out of my mouth and would deliver it to Jill later.

"That's really good," she said, writing down the first sentence.

"What's good?"

"That first sentence: 'A new day has dawned.' That's nice."

We smiled at each other. "Thanks," I said.

I waited for her to give me a signal that she was done. She nodded.

"We are now not just a government by the people—"

"This pen's out of ink."

"Oh. Here. Try mine."

As I bent down to give her the pen, I noticed that she smelled really good. When I backed away, we looked at each other, and I noticed something I'd never noticed before. She had freckles on her nose. Possibly the most perfectly circular freckles I'd ever seen.

"Okay, we are now a government of people . . ." she started.

"No, no. We are now not just a government by the people."

"Oh, I see. That's different. And a lot better."

"Thanks. But your way was good too."

● ● ●

No one was wasting any time using the money they'd received from the government. I strolled around town just to see if anything had changed, and there was more activity than there had been in months. The farmers were busy in their garden.

"What are you planting?" I asked them.

"Oh, just the standards. Cucumbers, beans, tomatoes, carrots, turnips."

The government was buying turnips from them?

They continued to hoe, looking very much like they knew what they were doing.

The Clean Up Kidsboro group was making a trash run. They had been at it for a couple of hours by the time I walked by, so they had pretty much cleared the entire town of any trash. But still they searched.

"The place looks really good," I said to Mark.

"I know," he replied. His eyes darted wildly as he continued to scan the ground.

"So, why are you still looking?"

He stopped suddenly and looked at me as if I had just told him I thought the capital of Florida was France. "Ryan, litter is thrown on the ground every two seconds in this country. This is not a one-time clean-up project. It is an ongoing quest. It is a lifestyle. Our land is too important to ignore for even one minute."

I felt like standing at attention and covering my heart. "Then by all means, get back to it," I said. I wanted to tell him that 27 people had littered while we were having that conversation, but I felt that would put too much pressure on him.

"Would you get that dog out of my house!" I heard someone yell from across town. It sounded like Valerie. I rushed over to her clubhouse. She was trying to drag a big German shepherd out of her house by the collar. "Get over here and get your dog!" she shouted. The dog's owner, Melissa, the leader of the animal rights group, came over slowly, as if to torture Valerie for as long as possible.

"Why do we have all these mangy animals here?" Valerie pointed to several dogs and cats being held by their owners. "They should be chained up."

"What?" Melissa said.

"They're a nuisance. We should have a law saying that if they're going to be here, they have to be chained up."

"No way!"

Valerie turned to me. "Ryan, I think you should bring this up at the next city council meeting."

"I guess I could."

"No!" Melissa shouted. "You gave animals equal rights. People aren't chained up. Why should animals have to be?"

"Um . . ."

"Oh, perfect. Nice decisive answer there, Ryan," Valerie said. "Meanwhile, this place has turned into a pound."

"Don't say 'pound' in front of them," Melissa said in a harsh whisper.

"If this dog gets into my house again, I'm grabbing one of those slingshots," she said, pointing away from us.

I looked in the direction she was pointing, and saw that the slingshot boys were meeting in a group not too far from the dogs and cats. They were comparing their equipment, and every now and then, they would fling a nut away from town. I could tell the animal owners were getting nervous with these flying nuts, even though it looked like the slingshotters were being careful. Scott was with them, looking anxious to learn some slingshot skills.

A squirrel ran by, and I saw one boy aim at it but stop as soon as he saw me looking at him. Or maybe it was just my imagination. The animal rights group was keeping a close eye on the slingshotters.

The groups may not have been getting along with each other, but they were all happy about getting the chance to do something they believed in. I was proud I'd given them the opportunity, but now came the hard part: collecting taxes.

FIVE

REALITY SETS IN

A FEW WEEKS BEFORE the budget debate, we had passed out an income tax form to all residents of Kidsboro. Everyone was supposed to keep good records of the money they had made over the year. People could try to lie, but in a town as small as Kidsboro, it was hard to hide how much money was spent where. We had records of most transactions.

When we added up everyone's salary and how much the new budget was going to cost, we figured out that the tax rate for this year had to be 19 percent. I knew this was a little high, but we had a lot of new programs to pay for. People were not going to be very happy about having to give up 19 percent of everything they made, but it was something that had to be done, and they all knew it was time for sacrifice.

When we came up with the 19 percent figure in the city council meeting, Nelson had almost fainted. He would have to fork over a huge amount of money. "I'm so glad I'm paying for vegetables I'm not gonna eat and a bathroom I'm not gonna use," he said as he stormed out.

We calculated what everyone would have to hand over, and then Alice and I went door-to-door to collect. Usually she went alone, since she had no trouble squeezing money out of people—sometimes literally—by herself. But I went along this time to offer an explanation.

The first door we knocked on was Roberto's. Roberto was Jill's assistant at the *Chronicle*. He usually had very little to say about anything. But he had yet to see how much he owed.

"Eleven starbills?" he asked.

"Yes. That's what you owe in taxes for the year," I told him.

"I don't have that much money," he said with a Hispanic accent.

"I'm sorry, that's why we told everyone to save up. This is tax day."

"I don't understand the taxes."

"The tax rate is 19 percent, which means you owe the government 11 starbills. This was all explained in the memo we sent out to everyone."

"I cannot pay that much."

"Then we may have to set you up on a payment plan. Give us what you have now."

"I have nothing."

"You don't have anything?"

"No."

"Well . . . then . . . you'll have to give us your full salary every week until you pay us back."

"My full salary?"

"Yeah. How much do you make?"

"About three starbills in two weeks."

"Okay, then it'll take about nine weeks for you to pay off your taxes."

"Oh," he said, the impact of this finally dawning on him, "almost the whole summer."

I wasn't sure what to say. I'd always liked Roberto. He had been compliant with all our laws, he worked hard at the *Chronicle*, and he was a model citizen. I wanted to give him a break, but that would've been unfair. I wouldn't be giving a break to anyone else.

"Thank you very much," he said, disappearing into his clubhouse. His shoulders were sagging.

Alice and I looked at each other. We had to do this 33 more times.

● ● ●

After crushing the hopes and dreams of 34 people, I went back to my office to take a break. Jill walked in as soon as I closed the door behind me.

"What is this?" she asked before she was even all the way inside. She was holding up a piece of paper.

"What is what?"

"Were you sleepwalking when you wrote this press release?"

"What do you mean?"

"It's got all sorts of spelling errors and incomplete sentences. I can't even tell what you're trying to say sometimes."

"Oh," I said with a slight chuckle. "That's my new secretary . . . er . . . administrative assistant."

"Administrative assistant?"

"Yeah, this was her first dictation. She's still learning."

"Why do you need an assistant?"

"I've got a lot of paperwork. And it's a government job."

"Who is it?"

Right on cue, Lauren walked in with a handheld pencil sharpener. "I'm having . . . oh, I'm sorry. I didn't know you had a visitor. Hi, Jill."

"Lauren? You're his new assistant?"

"Yes. It's a great job, very challenging."

"Really?"

"Ryan, I'm done sharpening pencils," Lauren said. She handed over a shoebox full of sharp pencils.

"Thank you. Good job."

We looked at each other as she moved away. She briefly touched my arm and said, "Thanks. You're welcome."

"No problem."

I watched her leave the room. She gave me a little wave as she turned out. Jill had her hands on her hips. "Lauren's your assistant?"

"She'll be fine. She just needs some time."

"I'm so glad my tax dollars are being used this well."

● ● ●

Ten minutes after Jill left, Scott walked in. He was wearing his detective outfit—a Sherlock Holmes coat with matching hat, a magnifying glass sticking out of his pocket, and a bubble pipe that he claimed helped him think when he was on a case. I figured he was on one right now.

"What are you doing?" I asked.

"I'm on a case."

"What case?"

"I talked to Jake this morning at Whit's End. He told me that he wasn't the one who spilled the information about you to the *Barnacle*."

"Yeah. Right," I said sarcastically.

"Pardon me for walking the earth, but don't you think that's weird? I mean, if Jake really did do it, wouldn't he love to tell everyone? He would love it if everyone knew he'd exposed you."

That was true.

"Plus, you let him into Kidsboro because he knew about your past. That's how he got you to do everything for him— blackmail. So why would he play the only card he had? Seems like he would've tried to hold on to it to get something else out of you."

Maybe the bubble pipe really did work; all of this made sense. "Who else could it be? No one else knew that stuff."

"I don't know, but it could be worth some investigation. I say we head over to the *Barnacle*."

I was tired of thinking about taxes and the budget, so I decided to follow him. I couldn't imagine that we would turn up anything.

● ● ●

The *Barnacle* office was a regular clubhouse, only bigger than any of the ones in Kidsboro. Max Darby was King of Better-town, and he wanted his town to be bigger and better than Kidsboro in every possible way.

For whatever reason, there were very few people in town. On most days, tourism was high, and the place was buzzing with activity. *Maybe they're all someplace shedding their skins*, I thought to myself with a mischievous grin.

Scott knocked on the door of the *Barnacle*, but no one answered. Neither of us heard any rustling inside, so Scott took a quick glance around to see if anyone was looking, and then he opened the door.

I followed him but immediately protested, "This is breaking and entering."

"I'm just visiting the newspaper office."

"Max will hang me if we get caught breaking a law on his turf!"

"Don't worry about it. We'll be in and out in 10 seconds." He scanned the room. It was littered with papers—all over the desk, on the floor, tacked to the walls. A filing cabinet in the corner was half open. I had no idea what we were looking for, but Scott seemed to think the filing cabinet was a good place to start.

He opened one drawer and flipped through the labeled tabs on top. "Nothing," he said, moving on to the next drawer.

I scanned the table. There were handwritten notes on yellow sticky paper everywhere. The notes said things like "Kidsboro police corruption," "Kidsboro lawyers corrupt," and "Judge Amy paid off?" The *Barnacle* specialized in scandal.

"Bingo," Scott said in true TV-detective fashion. He pulled out a file labeled "Cummings" and leafed through it.

He gave me a stack of papers from inside and took the rest himself. I didn't hesitate to look at it, even though this was surely illegal.

"Look at this," Scott said. "Notes from the interview."

"Let me see that."

He turned so we could look at it together. It was hard to read the chicken scratch. It looked as if someone had written quickly to keep up with someone talking. It was a list of random facts about me. I read some of the things that appeared in the article—where I lived, my real name, the names of my pets . . . Wait a minute.

"Something's wrong," I said. "There's information here that wasn't in the article."

"They probably decided not to print everything."

"The name of my cat when I was little is in here."

"Not very print-worthy."

"This is impossible. The cat was dead before I ever knew Jake. He couldn't have known about it."

"Did you ever talk about your cat?"

"I was three. I barely remember it. I doubt I ever mentioned it, and if I did, I can't imagine Jake remembering it."

I scanned more of the page. "There's more stuff in here that he couldn't have known."

"So you don't think it was Jake?" Scott asked.

"Not unless he talked to my dad."

"Does he know where your dad is?"

I shook my head. "Nobody does."

"Then who?"

I stormed out of the *Barnacle*, not caring who saw me. We had to find the writer of that article. I just might have punched the wrong guy.

● ● ●

The reporter's name wasn't on the article. The *Barnacle* kept its authors secret because if the facts in the article were proven incorrect, which they almost always were, then the person who was offended by the article didn't know who to be mad at. But I did know the editor: a boy named Leo, who'd been a citizen of Bettertown since it began the previous fall. He had wanted to be a citizen of Kidsboro, but all he'd wanted to do was be the editor of a newspaper. There were no openings at the *Kidsboro Chronicle* since Jill was already the editor and she had a reporter, Roberto. So when Bettertown opened up, Leo pounced on the opportunity, even though working for the *Barnacle* meant he would have to publish garbage. I don't think this was what he really wanted, but in Bettertown, everybody did what Max told them to do, or they were thrown out. Leo had started the *Barnacle* reluctantly, but I got the feeling that he was starting to enjoy publishing scandals because the articles were getting more and more mean.

We found Leo at Whit's End, talking to Eugene Meltsner. Eugene was trying to work on a computer program, and Leo was obviously interrupting him. Leo was holding his reporter's notebook—a legal pad of paper exactly like the kind we'd found in my file at the *Barnacle*.

"Yes, he conceives of all of the inventions himself,"

Eugene said, agitated. "I simply assist him in the process of research and development."

"So, all he comes up with are the ideas?" Leo asked.

"No, we work together. I believe we went over this once already."

"I just find it hard to believe that a 12-year-old kid could come up with some of this stuff on his own."

He was obviously trying to dig up dirt on Nelson.

Eugene had clearly had enough. "I apologize if I cannot give you the answer that you want. The truth is all that I can offer you." He looked at us as if we might be able to save him.

"Hey, Leo," I said. "I need to talk to you."

"What do you want?" he asked sharply. I don't think he'd ever forgiven me for not letting him into Kidsboro.

"Did you write that article about me?"

"Sorry. Can't reveal that information."

"Why not?"

"*Barnacle* policy."

"Who wrote the policy?"

"Me," he said with pride.

"Then you can change it. I need to know who wrote that article."

"Never mind, Ryan," Scott jumped in. "Come here." He motioned for me to follow him, and we walked 10 feet away, out of earshot.

"Leo wrote it," he whispered.

"How do you know?"

"While you guys were talking, I checked out the notes on that legal pad he's holding. Same handwriting as we saw on that paper at the *Barnacle*." Scott's detective agency really should have been more successful. The kid had a knack for this stuff.

We walked back over to Leo, armed with this new information. "I need to know who you interviewed to get that story."

"I thought you knew it was Jake."

"Well, now I know it wasn't."

"You mean you punched the guy in the face for nothing?"

"Yes. Could you at least tell me if I'm right? It wasn't Jake, was it?"

"No can do. A good reporter never gives away his source."

"A good reporter? That's what you call yourself?" Scott said. I gave Scott a sharp look. We were trying to convince him to help us; insulting him wouldn't help matters.

"How about this," Scott said. "I was at Miller's Ravine a month ago when Charlie Metzger got hurt. Tell us what we want to know, and I'll give you an interview and tell you everything."

"That's right. You were there, weren't you?"

"Yep."

A month before, Charlie Metzger and Scott had been playing around at Miller's Ravine, and Charlie fell in and had to go to the hospital. But the rumor got around school that it wasn't an accident, because just the day before Charlie's fall, he had told on Rodney Rathbone, leader of the worst gang in Odyssey, the Bones of Rath. Rodney got into trouble with the school principal, so after he found out that Charlie had ratted on him, everyone expected Rodney to seek revenge. Of course, when Charlie had to go to the hospital, word got around that the Bones of Rath did it, even though Scott was there and told the doctors that it was an accident. But the kids at school didn't believe Scott or Charlie, thinking that the two were just making up the story because they feared that the Bones of Rath would come after them again.

Scott had told me the whole story of how Charlie had simply slipped and fell. Now he was using the incident to tempt Leo to give away his information about me.

"You'll tell me everything?" Leo said.

"Everything," Scott replied. Of course, Leo didn't realize that Scott had already told everyone everything. This article would definitely be weak.

Leo licked his lips, scanned the room to see if anyone was watching, and then let it all spill. "The guy I interviewed was a reporter for the *Odyssey Times*."

"The guy that's been asking people about Kidsboro?" I asked.

"That's the one. We traded stories. He gave me the story about you, and I answered questions about Kidsboro. Now, give me the scoop, Scott."

"Later, I promise," he called out as we rushed off.

● ● ●

The *Odyssey Times* was a maze of gray cubicles, copy machines, and wastebaskets filled with bad ideas. I only knew one person at the *Times*—Dale Jacobs, the editor. I figured he was busy, but we would wait for him to have a quiet moment.

He was in a glassed-in office along the back wall. I could see him inside. He was on the phone and the door was closed. I waved, and he lifted a finger to tell us that he would be with us in a minute. We waited outside on a bench. A secretary approached us. "Can I help you?"

"I just need to ask Mr. Jacobs a question," I said.

"Does he know you?"

"Yes. My name's Ryan Cummings."

"I'll tell him you're here."

"Thank you."

Ten minutes later, Mr. Jacobs poked his head out the door of his office. "Hi, Ryan, Scott. Did you guys need me for something?"

"Just to ask one question. Who's doing the story on Kidsboro?"

"What story?"

"There was a reporter in Kidsboro a little while ago, asking questions. I figured you were doing a story on us."

"I've been thinking about doing a story on Kidsboro, but I haven't assigned a reporter to it yet."

Scott piped up. "Could a reporter do a story on his own, without you knowing about it?"

"If a reporter was doing the story for us, I would know about it."

Scott and I exchanged confused looks.

"What makes you think this person was from the *Odyssey Times*?" Mr. Jacobs asked.

I had never thought about that possibility. What if this person was not really a reporter? Maybe it was someone who was just trying to get information about me. But who would know all of that stuff about my past? There were only two people—my mom, who I knew wouldn't reveal any of that stuff . . . and my dad.

Could my dad be in Odyssey?

"What did he look like?" I asked Scott.

"The reporter?"

"Yeah."

"Um . . . he had black, spiky hair, kind of short. And he had a mustache."

I breathed a sigh of relief. My dad had red hair and was rather tall.

"No," Mr. Jacobs said. "That doesn't fit the description of anybody here."

It didn't fit the description of anyone I knew either. Who could it be?

SIX

THE DANGEROUS
REUNION

As MUCH AS I DESPISED the thought, I knew there was something I had to do before I returned to Kidsboro.

I found Jake at Whit's End again. He was sitting in a booth with Max. He saw me approach and sat up in his seat. Maybe he was expecting me to deck him again. I stopped in front of him.

"What do you want?" he growled.

"You didn't leak my story."

"I know."

"I thought you did," I said, hating every minute of this. "I was wrong. I shouldn't have hit you. I'm sorry."

"How considerate of you, Jim. You always were the polite one on our street. My mother always said, 'Why can't you be nice like Jim Bowers?' I always told her that no one can be nice like Jim Bowers. Jim Bowers is not real. Jim is fictional. Hitting me in the face was the only real thing you've ever done. In a weird way, I was proud of you."

"I didn't come here to be made fun of; I came here to ask for your forgiveness."

"Oh, I'll more than forgive you. I'll shake your hand in congratulations. I mean, I won't forget what you did. I'll definitely get you back for that. But I congratulate you because you deserve congratulations. You split open my chin. Let's just say I was impressed."

I turned around and headed for the door. I wasn't really expecting the forgiveness part, but the apology had to happen. As humiliating as that had been, at least now I could get on with my life.

● ● ●

The moment I stepped onto Kidsboro property, I could hear an argument going on. Then I saw three people outside Nelson Industries, yelling at each other. Nelson was one of them.

"I was here until six o'clock every night last week!" said one boy.

"I know. I'm sorry," Nelson replied.

"We had a contract!" the other boy said.

"There was no contract," Nelson argued.

"Well, there was an understanding!"

"Look, I'm sorry. I just can't afford you anymore," Nelson said.

"You can't afford two more employees?"

"Not with so much of our profits going to taxes."

"You could keep us on if you really wanted to."

"No, I can't. I've crunched the numbers every way I know how. I simply can't afford four employees anymore."

"Great."

"Listen," Nelson said, pleading, "maybe I'll be able to hire you back someday. You'll be the first people I call."

"No, thanks. I'd like a job that I can count on."

The two boys left. I didn't want to look Nelson in the face, because I knew he would blame this on me.

"You had to fire them?" I asked.

"Yes."

I knew this would be devastating for them. Working for Nelson Industries was one of the best jobs anyone could have. Nelson was always very fair in paying his employees.

"I can't pay the taxes," Nelson said, glaring at me, then turning to his two remaining employees. "Okay, guys. We've got work to do."

"Are you kidding me?" One of them said. "We could barely keep up with all the orders with five of us. Now we have to do it with only three?"

"Don't worry about it. With everyone else in town having to pay taxes too, there've been cancellations." He glanced at me one more time, and then disappeared into his clubhouse.

This was bad. Nelson Industries was the most successful business in town. If it was in trouble, the whole town was in trouble.

● ● ●

A crowd of people was gathered on the edge of town, and I ran over to see what was going on. Joey, the African-American preacher at Kidsboro Community Church, was on the ground in the middle of a two-layered circle of people. I could barely see him through their legs.

"What's going on?" I asked whoever might be listening.

"Joey's been blinded!" came the reply from an unknown source.

"What?" I scrambled in between the bodies and made it to the center where James, the doctor, was trying to look at Joey's eye, while Joey was covering it with his hand. There was blood on the top of Joey's shirt and on the back of his hand.

"What happened?" I demanded.

"He was hit in the eye by a rock," said James, the expert at the scene.

"It's not my eye," Joey said, without looking up. "It's my forehead."

"Let me see, Joey," I said, kneeling down.

"I'll move my hand if he promises not to touch me," Joey said, pointing to James.

"Step back, James," I said.

"I took a first aid course!" James shouted. "I know what I'm doing!"

"Just step back."

James rolled his eyes and moved back six inches on his haunches. Joey lifted his hand. The crowd pressed in to get a closer look. There was a gash above his left eye. It had bled some but was stopped for now.

"Does anybody have a tissue or something?"

"I've got bandages!" James yelled before anyone else could even process the question. He opened his black doctor bag, and, for the first time in his medical career, he was able to use something from it for a real medical purpose. In two seconds he'd found a package of sterile gauze and flipped it to me.

I carefully opened the package and gave the gauze to Joey. "Just press this against the wound. It may need stitches. We should get you to a doctor." Looking up I said, "Somebody go to Whit's End and call his mom."

I heard someone run off. "Come on, Joey." I helped him up. He swayed a little bit when he got to his feet, as if he were dizzy, so I didn't push him too fast.

"Okay, how was he hit with a rock?" I asked the crowd.

"Slingshot," said Scott, who I now noticed was part of the crowd.

I felt my face get hot. "Whose?"

"Ben's."

"It was an accident," I heard Ben say. "It got away from me."

"This is not a designated slingshot area."

"It was *shot* from one," he said. "It just didn't *land* in one."

"That's no excuse," Pete, the lawyer said. He stepped to the front of the crowd. "This is an outrage. Joey, you need to sue this man!" he said, pointing to Ben.

"We don't need this, Pete," I said.

"Joey's gonna need stitches. He's entitled to damages."

"Stop it!"

Pete turned to Joey. "You could sue this pea brain for all he's worth."

"Hey!" shouted Ben. "Get outta here."

"I'm not going anywhere, Ben. And I would suggest you get your own lawyer."

Ben made a swim move past two bodies in front of him and came at Pete. Pete dropped his briefcase and lifted his arms to defend himself. Ben pushed him, sending Pete sprawling to the ground.

"Stop!" I shouted.

"Come on, Pete," Ben yelled. "You want to sue somebody? How much do you think you can get if I break both your arms?" The crowd egged both of them on.

Pete didn't get up. "Oh, real smart. Pushing me in front of 15 witnesses. I could take you for everything."

Ben moved to kick him, and I stepped in front. "Ben!" Scott and I grabbed him and pulled him back. He wasn't a very big guy, so it wasn't terribly difficult to get him away from the scene.

"That's it!" I shouted. "Ben, go home and take your slingshot with you. Pete, no one's suing anybody. You can go home too. Everybody, mind your own business. I'm taking Joey to Whit's End now."

I turned to Joey, who didn't seem to be taking any of this in. "You okay?" He nodded. "Ready to go?" He nodded again.

I put my arm around him and led him away. As we walked away, I turned around briefly. The crowd had not dispersed. They just stared at the two of us. I couldn't tell if they were concerned for Joey, or if they blamed me for the whole thing happening in the first place.

• • •

We met Joey's mother at Whit's End. Mr. Whittaker looked at the wound and kept pressure on it until he was ready to go. Then Joey's mom took him to the doctor.

When I got back into town, there was still an uneasy buzz in the air. The walls of a strong city were beginning to crumble, and it felt like it was only the beginning.

I picked up a copy of the *Kidsboro Chronicle*, which had just come out, and skimmed through the first few pages. There was a lot about the changes the city council had made, as well as the effects of the changes. Jill had written the articles and usually she was very fair in her writing. But there was an edge to these, as if she disagreed with every decision that had been handed down. I knew this couldn't be true, though, because she had been involved in those decisions herself.

I turned the page and discovered that I wasn't imagining things. The headline on the editorial page was "Mayor and City Council Give In to Special Interests," by Jill Segler. What? Give in?

In the article, she took responsibility for herself in saying that she was a member of the city council, and she'd made a mistake when she allowed the budget to pass. But she kept referring to it as "the mayor's proposal" and "the mayor's budget plan." One line that particularly bothered me was, "The mayor's budget plan ignored the true needs of the city in order to please a few people." She went on to criticize "the mayor's decision to hire an assistant that he doesn't need."

I couldn't read on. I threw the paper down and stormed over to the newspaper office. I pushed open the door without knocking. Jill was sitting at her desk.

"What are you doing?" I asked harshly.

"You think you're the first political leader to get criticized in the press?" she replied calmly.

"But those things you wrote—"

"Were all true."

"Mine was not the only vote in the city council."

"I messed up too, but it's your name on the budget proposal."

"You're on the city council. You're supposed to back me up."

"I have to print the truth. There's no loyalty in journalism."

"What kind of a motto is that?"

"I have a responsibility to my readers to print the truth. We caved in to all those groups. Slingshots? Vegetables? Why are we paying for these things? And why do you need an assistant?"

"You're a supporter of the group that wanted me to create more government jobs for girls. You wanted me to hire an assistant!"

"But why did you listen to me?"

I was all ready with my next response, but her question caught me by surprise. All I could come up with was a quiet "What?"

"You used to be strong. You used to stand up to people. You didn't care about popularity or making everybody happy. You did what you thought was best. I don't know what happened to you, but you'd better find your spine or this town is going down the tubes."

I was quieter, but no less angry. "You didn't have to vote for this proposal. I wrote it, and I handed it to you. This town is just as much your responsibility as it is mine. If I'm going down, you're going with me. I'm writing a rebuttal to your article, and I expect you to print it."

I didn't wait for her to respond. I left, slamming the door behind me. Smoke was coming out my ears. She was irresponsible, thoughtless, reckless, wishy-washy . . .

And right.

● ● ●

I was still going to write my rebuttal, even though in my heart, I knew Jill's article was accurate. I just wanted to deflect some of the blame off of me.

I sat down at my desk and pulled out a pencil and my notebook. Lauren had noticed me walking by and poked her head in. "Do you need me for anything?"

"No, thanks."

"You want me to take dictation?"

"No, I'll just write this one by myself." I wondered if she had read the article and wanted to make sure that I still felt like I needed her. Not that her actions were any different than they had been in the weeks before. She had been a faithful, helpful employee.

She backed out of my office, and I got down to writing. Halfway through my first sentence, I suddenly became distracted. There was a feeling in the air that was so strong it forced me to stand up. My stomach dropped like the time I woke up and thought I heard someone breaking into the house. There was an intruder nearby. Obviously, he wasn't inside right then. It was a small clubhouse and there was nowhere for anyone to hide. But there was a presence there, and I could almost feel it choking me. It was a sense . . . or a smell . . . or . . .

I backed up against the wall, suddenly needing air desperately. I had to prop myself up with the desk as I anxiously moved for the door. I lunged out. Lauren was sitting at a desk outside my door. I was gasping.

"What's wrong?" she asked.

"I . . . I'm just going for a walk." But walking wouldn't do the trick. After a few steps, I found myself running. I headed straight for home, the feeling of dread melting away with every stride. I ran out of breath, not from running, but from this strange horror that had overtaken me. I slowed down and caught my breath. The feeling was gone. I wasn't being strangled anymore, and I felt like I could breathe again.

Was I going crazy?

● ● ●

I went home. It was much earlier than usual for me to go home for the day, but I didn't want to be anywhere near my clubhouse. I figured I would go up to my room and read for a while. I'd get lost in another world for an hour or two, and I'd forget the one I had just run from.

"Mom?" I called out when I opened the back door and went into the kitchen. She didn't answer, and I remembered that she'd had an afternoon meeting at work. I opened the refrigerator and pulled out some orange juice. As I reached for a glass, I felt a draft. I was suddenly very aware of sounds outside—birds, cars driving by on the street. I peered into the living room and saw that a window was open. Strange, I thought, since the air conditioning was on. The thin drapes were billowing in the wind. I closed the window.

As soon as the wood of the window touched the wood of the sill, I felt it again—the same presence I'd felt in my clubhouse. The cup dropped from my hand as my entire body went numb.

It finally hit me which sense was being heightened—the sense of smell. There was a familiar scent in the air: the smell of dread and fear and a time I wanted to forget. I managed to move my legs enough to maneuver past the dining room table and toward the stairs. I was walking in slow motion, dreading each step but desperately wanting to know who or what was there in my house, alone with me.

I heard and saw nothing. But the smell was getting stronger. It sickened me but also drew me. I walked on, my eyes darting but my head not moving, for fear that I would make a noise and awaken something I wanted to remain asleep. As I started up the stairs, something caught my eye. On an end table by the couch was a set of keys. Not my mom's keys, not my keys . . . but a set of keys with a picture-frame keychain on it. Taking a closer look, I saw that in the picture frame was a photo of me—when I was seven.

I whipped around and headed for the door. Frantically, I scrambled for the doorknob, but my sweaty hands slipped off it. Trying to unlock the door was suddenly like trying to disarm a bomb before it went off.

"Jim."

I screamed and threw myself against the wall in one motion. It was my dad. I tried to scream again but nothing came out. He was just standing there, 15 feet away, smiling but obviously nervous. I pressed myself against the wall harder, trying to put as much distance between him and me as possible.

"I'm sorry. I didn't mean to scare you. I didn't think you'd be home yet. I thought you'd stay in Kidsboro longer."

He looked exactly the same except for a few things. He had dyed his hair black, probably because he was a fugitive from the law, and, for some reason, he seemed much shorter than he had before. Maybe because the last time I had seen him *I* was much shorter.

He appeared sober, and that was encouraging. He also didn't move toward me, which made me feel better. But he had always been very good at getting people to trust him.

Tears welled up in his eyes. "You're so big. You look just like I did at your age."

My lips were trembling, but I managed a question. "Why are you here?"

"Well, I know you're not gonna believe this, but . . . I missed you. I wanted to see my family again. I promise I won't hurt you. I know you've heard that before, Jim, but I've changed. Really. You guys leaving just killed me. I didn't even want to go on. There was a time when all I did was think about my life, and how I'd messed·it up so bad. So I turned to God, Jim. Just like you. About a year ago I became a Christian. Jesus helped me get back on my feet. I've stopped drinking, I've stopped . . . well, a lot of stuff. I have a new life now. I want the chance to prove to you that I've changed, because I want my family back."

I was still pressed up against the wall. "If you're a Christian," I said, "why did you break into our house?"

"I know I shouldn't have done that. But I wanted to know you again, and I was still scared that you wouldn't want to know me. That's why I went to Kidsboro and asked all those questions. I wanted to meet my boy again, even if it was through his friends. You've got some great friends, Jim. They love you. They think you're the best, even the ones who disagree with you. I'm so proud to be your father. Do you think it would ever be possible for you to forgive me for all I've done to you?"

I didn't move a muscle. He had convinced me many times before that he was a "new man," and I was always devastated when I soon realized that he wasn't. "I don't believe you," I said.

My dad closed his eyes and dropped his head. "I don't blame you."

When he closed his eyes, I subconsciously planned my escape. My hand drifted up toward the doorknob.

"I know we can never be a family again," he said, "but I'd like to be able to visit, you know? I don't know if I can handle being out of your life forever."

Our next door neighbor pulled into his driveway. My dad was distracted for a moment, maybe thinking it could be my mom. I saw an opening and took it. I bounded up the stairs and ran into Mom's room—the only inside door in the house with a lock.

"Jim!"

My heart was beating so loudly that I couldn't tell if there were footsteps behind me or not.

I burst through my mom's bedroom door and spun around to reach the lock. I slammed the door, knocking two pictures off the walls. I turned the lock and ran for the phone by her bed.

Mr. Henson was on speed-dial, so I punched two numbers and waited for his phone to ring.

It wasn't a dead-bolt lock, and it wasn't a steel door. I knew he could get in if he really wanted to. I watched the knob carefully, waiting for it to turn.

One ring.

It was happening just like it had before. When my dad was on a tirade, I would sit up in my room, huddled up on my bed. I would sit and wait for it to be over, praying to God that the door wouldn't open, and that he wouldn't turn his anger on me.

Two rings.

It felt like I had been on this phone for hours. *Please be there!* I heard a noise and locked my eyes on the knob. Still, it didn't turn. Maybe he was grabbing a bat or something to knock the door in. He might have been scouting the house out for days, he probably knew where my room was, and my closet, and . . .

I jerked my head around to the window. He could've

gone out my window and walked across on the porch roof! He could be right outside, ready to bash in the window with my aluminum bat.

"Hello?" It was Mr. Henson on the line.

"It's my dad. He's here in my house!"

"I'll be right there." I heard him yell to somebody, "Get over to the Cummings house! Now!" He came back on the line about 10 times calmer. "Where are you?"

"In my mom's bedroom."

"Where is he?"

"I don't know. I haven't heard anything since I ran away from him."

"So he knows you're there?"

"Yeah."

"Is the door locked?"

"Yes."

"Okay. Stay right where you are until we get there. Somebody should pull up in two minutes. Stay on the line."

I didn't know if I had two minutes. My eyes darted back and forth from the doorknob to the window, but I saw no signs of my dad. Outside the door, it was silent, as if I were alone. I didn't trust the silence.

Finally finding my head, I examined the room for an escape route in case he did come through the door. I could jump out the window, climb down the porch roof, and jump down into my front yard. Nothing else came to me, though I continued to scan. Then I saw the master bathroom. If I went in there and locked the door, it could buy me some time. If I only had to kill two minutes . . .

I glanced at my watch. I only cared about the second hand.

I thought I saw the doorknob move, but after 10 eternal seconds, decided it was my imagination.

My entire body was shaking, my shirt dripping with sweat. I checked my watch again. It had barely moved. I made a dash for the bathroom, ignoring Mr. Henson's orders to stay on the line.

I locked the door behind me and climbed into the bathtub. I was desperate for every second—perhaps the extra second it would take him to find me behind the shower curtain would be all I needed. I crouched down on the ceramic and bit my fingers.

Suddenly, off in the distance I could hear a siren. It was coming closer and closer . . . and then it stopped in front of my house.

I could hear at least two officers burst through the front door. One shouted something to the other, and I heard footsteps running up the stairs. An officer slammed his body on the bedroom door. "Is anyone in there?"

I managed a weak, "Yes." I jumped out of the tub and ran into the bedroom. I unlocked the door and let the officer in.

"Is he still here?" I asked.

"I don't think so. Did you see where he went?"

"No. I was running away from him."

"Was he armed?"

"I don't think so."

"How long were you up here?"

It seemed like four days. But I took a wild stab at the answer. "Maybe five or 10 minutes."

"How did he act? Was he angry?"

"No. He wanted me to forgive him."

"Okay, come on." He took me to the squad car. I sat in the back behind a locked door while three officers searched the house and all around it.

After they had searched everywhere, the officer who had come upstairs got into the front seat. "I'm gonna take you to your mother."

"Is anyone going to be looking for him?"

"We'll have a few squad cars and some officers on foot searching. We'll find him."

SEVEN

SHOCKING NEWS

My mom and I went to Mr. Whittaker's house. We were planning on staying with one of Mom's friends overnight, but we wanted to spend the evening with Mr. Whittaker. I always felt safe at his house.

He poured me a glass of lemonade. As I lifted the glass to my mouth, I noticed my hand was still shaking. We were silent for a long time, not really knowing what to say to each other.

"Do you think he's changed, Mom?" I finally asked.

"No," she said. I guess she saw my head drop, because she seemed to sense my disappointment. "Ryan, your father's very tricky. He's good at making people believe in him. But he always ends up disappointing them. I don't know if he could ever change."

I stared at my lemonade and asked the question again, only this time of Mr. Whittaker. "Do you think he could change?"

"God's changed worse people than your father, Ryan. I know it's possible. I hope your dad has changed, I really do.

But I understand how your mom feels. It would be tough to ever trust him again."

"Impossible, you mean," Mom interjected.

We sipped lemonade for a few more minutes, silent. "You do think they'll find him, don't you?" I asked.

"Yes, I do," Mr. Whittaker said. "He couldn't have gotten far."

"Because I don't want to move again," I said. "I like it here."

"I hope you don't have to move either."

• • •

I called Scott and told him I wouldn't be in Kidsboro the next day, and that I was handing over the reins to him. He was to be the mayor for the day. He sounded way too excited. He asked me if he would get my salary for the day, and I said yes. He finally got around to asking me why I wasn't coming. I told him I was taking a personal day off from work.

• • •

Mom and I slept in the same room that night at her friend's house. I was on a sofa, and she got the bed. Actually, not much sleeping occurred at all. I laid awake almost all night, staring at the ceiling. Every now and then, I glanced over at Mom. She was pretty much doing the same thing. There was a tree branch hitting the window outside. I knew it was a tree, but I still had trouble convincing myself of that. In my imagination, it was always my father trying to break in. If he could track us down to Odyssey, he could find us here. In fact, he could probably find us anywhere. I knew we'd have to go into hiding again, but I couldn't imagine ever feeling safe, no matter where we were.

"Ryan, are you awake?" Mom called softly.

"Yeah."

"I've been thinking. I hate it, but if they don't catch him, we're going to have to move again. Maybe to Canada or something."

I didn't want to hear those words, but I'd known they were coming. "I know."

"I'm sorry," she said.

"It's not your fault."

After a few moments of silence, I could hear her crying. I got off the sofa and snuggled up to her. She put her arm around my head and stroked my hair, we prayed together, and, finally, I was able to sleep.

● ● ●

It felt like I had just fallen asleep when there was a knock at our door. Mom's friend poked her head in the room we were staying in. "Hey." We both woke up. "There's a policeman here to see you."

It wasn't quite daylight yet, and I looked at the clock—5:54. This had to be important. We ran up the stairs and met the policeman just inside the front door.

"Sorry to wake you up, but I thought you should know this as soon as you could," he said.

"That's okay. What's going on?"

"We have your husband in custody. He's in the Richland jail right now." My mom gasped and covered her mouth with her hand. She hugged me as tightly as she ever had. I felt a hot tear running down my face. It was as if an anchor had just been unchained from my heart.

After we'd cried on each other for a few moments, Mom talked with the policeman. "How did you catch him?" she asked.

"We didn't," he said. "He turned himself in."

"Really?" I said. "He must've known there was no way out."

The policeman shook his head. "That wasn't it. He turned himself in in Richland, which is about two hours away from here. He must've caught a ride or hopped on a bus or something. We probably wouldn't have caught him all the way out there. He could have gotten off scot-free."

My mom looked at the officer as if his nose had just melted off his face. I must have looked the same way because he said, "You folks need to sit down?" We were too numb to move.

"What did he confess to?" Mom asked.

"Enough to keep him in prison for quite a while."

"I can't believe it."

"He's at the Richland sheriff's office if you want to go see for yourselves. A lot of folks want that."

"Yes," Mom said. "I think I need to see him behind bars for myself."

• • •

We took our time getting ready, even though I think Mom was anxious to get on the road for the two-hour trip. We ate breakfast, got dressed, and walked out the door into the bright sunlight. I noticed that Mom didn't put on any makeup, and though she may not have thought about it herself, I considered this important. My dad always wanted her to wear lots of makeup. Now she was going to see him for the first time in five years, and she didn't care anything about what she looked like to him. He was not going to tell her what to do anymore. Or maybe her mind was in other places and she forgot. I liked the first reason better.

We didn't talk much on the road. My head was filled with all sorts of emotions—mainly just relief. I couldn't believe it was finally over. But I was also a bit confused by the whole thing. As the road flew by, I came up with a theory.

"Mom," I said, the first word out of either of our mouths in 20 minutes.

"Yes?"

"Dad said something to me in the living room, and I was just thinking about it."

"What did he say?"

"He said that he wanted to prove to me that he had changed. Do you think maybe this was his way of doing that?"

"Turning himself in?"

"Yeah."

"Could be."

"I mean, why would he go all the way to Richland to turn himself in? I think he was trying to show us that he did it because he wanted to, not because he had to."

"You may be right."

She turned left and merged onto the interstate. There was little traffic. "Do you think he's changed?" I asked.

She chuckled under her breath, but then seemed to think it over. She glanced at me with sympathy. "You'd like that, wouldn't you? To know he had changed?"

"Yeah, sure."

"Why?"

"I guess . . . well, sometimes . . . I miss him."

She breathed a long, difficult breath. "Me too. And I wish he would change; I really do. But Ryan, I don't think there's anything he could do to prove it to me. There are just too many scars."

I adjusted myself in the seat and pretended I was very interested in the trees passing by the window. I didn't want her to see me cry.

• • •

An officer sat alone at a big desk at the sheriff's office. He seemed to be expecting us. "Ms. Cummings?"

"Yes."

"Why don't you come on back with me?"

We followed him through a steel door and back into a damp, concrete-walled area that felt like my uncle's unfinished basement. Along the far wall were two jail cells—one empty and one holding my father. I could see Dad stand up from his cot. We approached him slowly as the officer pulled two chairs over from the opposite wall. He placed them in front of the cell for my mom and me, and then stood by the door. I was glad he was there. Mom pulled her chair back a little farther away from the cell, and then sat down.

Dad gave a half-smile to Mom. "You look nice." She didn't answer. "Both of you look so nice." I didn't answer either. After an awkward pause, he stepped toward the bars and leaned against them. "I did some research last week at the law library. With all the stuff I've done, it looks like I'll get a minimum of five years." He smiled, probably wondering if we wished it were more. "Guess that'll give me some time to think. . . . Give you guys some time to think too."

"I don't need any time to think," Mom said, stone-faced. She sat up straight in her chair, seemingly determined not to show any emotion but complete indifference.

"I understand that. I do. I can't blame you for all the things you feel about me right now. I'm not expecting any miracles. Maybe just a letter every now and then." He pressed his face between two bars and looked at us like a puppy dog about to be left in the pound. "I miss you so much."

There was another awkward pause. He studied us. I guess Mom had gotten her closure—she saw him behind bars and was satisfied—because she stood up quickly and scooted her chair back against the wall. "I'm ready to go. Come on, Ryan."

Seeing him behind bars was not what I came to do, though. I wasn't through yet, and I didn't quite know why. "Can I stay for a few minutes?"

She looked surprised that I'd asked, but then softened for the first time since we had walked through the door. "I'll be out here," she said, and without looking at Dad again, she headed out.

The heavy door clanged shut behind her, leaving only Dad and me and the police officer. I had no idea what to say and was grateful when Dad finally started talking. "Do you hate me?" he asked, his face looking as if he were preparing for someone to punch him.

"Sometimes," I said. "But not right now."

He chuckled a little bit. "I guess I'll take what I can get. Do you know why I turned myself in?"

"Why?"

"Because I didn't care about anything. I didn't care about being stuck behind bars for five years; I didn't care if I never made another dime; I didn't care if I ever lived another day in the sun. The only thing I wanted was a chance to be your dad again, and I knew you'd never let me do that unless there were steel bars between us. And at least five years for both of us to think about . . . each other." He ducked his head and pressed his hair against the bars, looking at the ground.

"I'm so proud of you. The way you've grown. You're so smart and kind and . . . I was actually kind of jealous talking to your friends in Kidsboro, because you've got something now that I never had: respect. You've made enough good decisions that people respect you. I never made any good decisions—always selfish ones." He lifted his head and looked at me again. "Don't ever lose that, Jim. Don't ever do anything that would make others lose respect for you. Trust is a hard thing to get. Pretty easy to lose, though. Look at me. I'm gonna be working a lifetime trying to get you to trust me again. It may take even longer than that."

"It may not take as long as you think," I said. His eyes gleamed a bit. It was probably his first ray of hope in a long time. "I'll write to you, Dad."

"I'd like that. And I'll write to you, too."

I turned and looked at the door. "I'd better get going."

"Okay."

I scooted the chair against the wall and headed for the steel door.

"I love you," he said, again acting like he was waiting for someone to punch him. My lips formed the words to tell him I loved him too, but they got stuck in the back of my throat. All I could manage was a nod and a smile. I pushed the door open and joined my mother.

EIGHT

THE GREATEST SHOW ON EARTH

I DIDN'T FEEL READY to go back to Kidsboro the next day, but I did want to do one thing. I went to the services at Kidsboro Community Church at least twice a month, mainly to show my support for Pastor Joey, who always tried hard to say something meaningful.

Mr. Whittaker attended services almost every week and sat in the same place: front row on the right. I saw him before he sat down. "How's your mom?" he asked.

"She's not ready to have a party yet, but she's getting there. She's taking off work for a few days."

"Good. I've been praying for you guys."

"I know. Thanks." He smiled and nodded, and then we sat down for the service.

There were only five of us there—Mr. Whittaker, myself, a young African-American boy whom I had never seen before, Marcy, who sat in the back, and Joey, who had a large bandage above his eye. "Healing okay?" Mr. Whittaker whispered, pointing to his head.

"Yeah." He'd had to get three stitches.

Joey started the service with announcements. He began reading from a sheet of paper. "We have choir rehearsal this Wednesday at 5:30. I could really use more tenors . . . and basses . . . and sopranos. Last week only one person showed up, so I guess we need just about anybody." Mr. Whittaker and I exchanged looks, wondering if we should volunteer for the choir.

"Also, we only had three people sign up for the church softball team. We really need more than that, especially if the other team hits any balls to the outfield. I put the sign-up sheet on the meeting hall bulletin board, but all I got were three names." He read the names off. "So far we have Lou Gehrig, Ken Griffey Junior, and Gen . . . Geng . . ." He showed the name to Mr. Whittaker to get help pronouncing it.

"Genghis Khan," Mr. Whittaker said, rolling his eyes.

"Thank you. Um . . . I don't know any of those people. If you happen to see them, they didn't put phone numbers down, so tell them we'll practice next week if we have enough people for a team."

I was sure Mr. Whittaker would give him the bad news later.

"Now, for the special music, my little brother Terry is going to play his xylophone."

The little boy that I'd never met before stood up and pulled out a toy xylophone. The mallet was attached by a string. Without looking up at anyone, he started playing the slowest version of "Amazing Grace" I had ever heard. He missed a few notes, but it was still very moving. After he played the last note, he slid the xylophone under his seat and sat down, still without looking at anyone. "Thank you, Terry," Joey said.

"Let's turn to Second Corinthians, chapter 11." I had forgotten my Bible, but Mr. Whittaker let me share his.

I couldn't imagine Joey ever winning any contests in public speaking. He did not have a very polished delivery, and his content usually sounded like it was meant for a five year old. But Joey had a knack for picking the right sermon at the right time. This time, as always, he had something to say to me personally.

"How many of you have heard of the apostle Paul?" he said, asking for a show of hands. His father, also a preacher, did this in his own sermons to get people's attention and to get them involved. Joey didn't do it with quite as much flair, but it did get us involved. Mr. Whittaker and I both raised our hands.

"Paul was a missionary for Jesus. And he had a real bad time of it. Wherever he went, he was in danger. He was beaten, robbed, and stoned. He was in three shipwrecks and thrown into jail a bunch of times. He hardly ever slept. He had to fight against lots of people who didn't want the gospel spread. But he did it anyway. He did what he had to do, even though it made him unpopular, sent him to jail, and all that other stuff.

"Like it says in First Peter 3:14, 'But even if you should

suffer for what is right, you are blessed.' Paul stood up for what was right," Joey said, "and he was blessed, because he became probably the greatest missionary ever and wrote more books of the Bible than anyone else."

Joey was right once again. The apostle Paul stood up for what was right, even though it made him unpopular. Suddenly it occurred to me that if you do the right things long enough, not only will God bless you, but you will win the respect of other people. I realized that my decisions should never be based on what I think will make me more popular. They should be based on what is right. I wanted to jump out of my chair and clap. I now knew what I had to do. Actually, there were two things I had to do. I would start on number one immediately.

● ● ●

I called everyone that I could find together. I grabbed people off the streets of Kidsboro and asked them to join me in the meeting hall. I was glad that Scott, Nelson, and Jill were among them.

They gathered at my invitation, and I stood in front of a lot of confused faces. This was something I'd wanted to do for five years.

"I called you all here to publicly apologize. I lied to each and every one of you, and I'm sorry. I ask for your forgiveness. I lied to you about my life in California because my mother and I had to escape my abusive father. We changed our names because we didn't want him to find us. I will answer any questions you ask, because now it's finally over.

My dad is in prison and will be there for a while." I scanned the faces and could sense that no one blamed me.

"My name is Jim Bowers, but that's a name I'd rather forget. I'd like you to keep calling me Ryan. Other than my name and my past, I'd like to believe I'm the same person you've always known me to be. Please don't treat me any differently."

I noticed Jill among the faces. I had promised her that someday I would reveal my deep secret. From the look on her face, I could tell that she forgave me, just like everyone else.

● ● ●

After the crowd cleared out, Jill approached me. "So that's your big secret."

"That's it."

"I was kind of hoping you were a criminal. It'd make better headlines."

I chuckled.

"Listen," she said. "I want to apologize for that nasty article I wrote about you."

"No, you were right," I said. "I caved in."

"I did too. We really made a mess of things, didn't we?"

"Yeah . . . but I don't think it'll last much longer."

"Why do you say that?"

"I have a plan. Let's get a city council meeting together."

● ● ●

The city council agreed on what we had to do. We had to make the special-interest groups accountable for the money we'd given them. We made appointments with all of them, and they all came, group by group, to hear the bad news. The five city council members sat on one side of a table, while the members of the different groups stood on the other side and heard their sentences.

"You have three days to prove to us that your group is good for our society and not dangerous," I said to the slingshot group. They looked worried. "We want to see the benefits of having slingshots in our town."

They all looked at each other as if to say, "Are there any benefits?" But they tried to act as confident as they could.

"We will have another meeting in three days—72 hours from right now—and if you can't prove that slingshots are truly useful, we will take away your designated slingshot area and make slingshots illegal again. Got it?"

They nodded slowly, and then realized they needed to look positive about finding benefits to having slingshots in Kidsboro. "No problem. Three days."

"We'll have lots of stuff by then."

"We don't even really need three days."

"I can already think of 10 or 12 benefits right off the top of my head."

We all waved good-bye, and as soon as they got out of earshot, we could see them having a panic meeting.

The other groups paraded in as well. The farmers were told that in three days we would check out their garden to see whether it was making progress, and they would also have to submit a written plan for making sure the produce was all eaten. They left arguing about who would write the plan. I don't think any of them really believed the vegetables would actually be eaten by people.

The animal rights group had to prove to us that their animals could contribute something positive to our city. If humans were required to take their places in society, then animals had to as well. They all had to find jobs in three days. I had a feeling that if any of the dogs became respected physicians, James would scream.

The Clean Up Kidsboro group had three days to show us that their goals were being accomplished. Otherwise, they would lose their funding. Kidsboro had to be virtually litter and pollution-free, and they had to make sure the outdoor bathroom was built.

"Who's going to build it?" one of the group members asked. I just smiled.

● ● ●

Valerie's feminist group came in, expecting us to start fulfilling our promises to them. They got what they asked for—sort of.

"I'm giving your group a government project."

Valerie and the two other girls high-fived each other.

"You will be paid, as a group, to build an outdoor bathroom."

"I'm sorry. A what?" Valerie said.

"An outdoor bathroom. A latrine."

"Oh."

"I thought you'd appreciate that since you said you wanted jobs that were usually given to boys," I told them.

They stared at me with their mouths open. They had to make a toilet?

"Okay," Valerie said, putting on a brave face. "We'll do it."

"Yes, you will," I said. "Because if it's not done in three days, you'll lose all your funding."

"Three days . . . great. We'll get right on it." This was supposed to be what they wanted. They had to be determined to do it.

They turned around, their eyes still wide with shock.

The feminist group was the last of the day, and the city council members began gathering up our things. Scott snickered, and Nelson joined him. All these groups had come in with their heads held high, and had left with their tails between their legs.

I was interested in seeing the results of this challenge. Scott and I planned to watch everyone very carefully. But there was one thing I had to do before I started. And I was dreading it.

● ● ●

"You called for me, Mr. Mayor?"

"Yes, Lauren. Have a seat, please," I told her.

She hesitated before she sat, as if she wondered if my asking her to sit was a sign that I was going to say something bad.

"You don't want to sit?" I asked.

"Did I do something wrong?"

"No."

"I've been working on my spelling, I really have."

"It's not your spelling."

"Is it something else I did?"

"You didn't do anything, Lauren. I just need to talk to you." She finally sat down, though she didn't look like she believed me.

"Lauren . . ." I knew immediately that I shouldn't have started off saying her name, because she closed her eyes and prepared for the blow. "You know that we've had some economic problems in Kidsboro lately."

"Yes."

"It's because of these new taxes. A lot of extra money is going out this year to different groups of people, and because we're having so many problems with the economy, the city council and I believe that we need to hold these groups accountable. You also know that I've been under some criticism for hiring you, right?"

She suddenly stood up and started crying. "I'll have my desk cleaned out this afternoon, Mr. Mayor."

"Lauren, I'm not firing you."

"You're not?"

"You have to pass a test. To prove that you're worth your salary."

"A test?"

"Yes. It's a project, and you have to have it done in three days."

"Okay," she said, wiping away the tears.

I pulled out a thick stack of papers. "This is the city charter. Every law that we've ever come up with for Kidsboro is in it. We've added a lot to it since we started, so it's very disorganized. There are laws stuck in here at random, and they need to be put in categories. Like laws that have to do with the court system, laws about conduct in the town, laws about money—stuff like that. It all needs to be retyped and look very professional by the time your three days are up." She had a blank look on her face. "Do you understand?" I asked.

She nodded slowly, but I wasn't convinced.

"I'm not allowed to give you help on this. It has to be your project."

She took the stack of papers and looked at it as if it were written in Swahili. I had sympathy for her. "I'm sorry."

"It's not your fault."

"Do your best."

"I will." She turned and headed for the door, hunched over like an old woman with a bad back.

This was a project that I felt would be challenging, but could be done by most people my age. I had serious doubts about Lauren being able to handle it, though. I felt like I had just given out my first pink slip.

● ● ●

Over the next two days, Scott and I ducked behind bushes and trees, watching the special-interest groups unravel like a bad sweater.

Valerie and her clan were gathered at the spot where they'd been told to build the bathroom. They all had their shovels out, but no one was digging. Scott and I crouched behind some bushes to listen to what they were saying.

"Come on, we have to do this," Valerie said.

"I think I'd be better at helping build the walls," Patty said.

"What's the big deal? It's just a hole."

"Yeah, but it's the thought of what it's going to be," another girl said. "And how are we going to be able to walk down the halls of our school ever again? Everybody'll call us the Toilet Girls."

"Yeah," Patty agreed.

"It's just gross."

"Nobody will even come near us."

"I can't do it."

"Okay, okay," Valerie said. "This is silly. We need to do it. This will prove once and for all that we're equal to boys—that we can do anything they can do. There's nothing in there but dirt. We don't have to ever use it, we just have to dig it."

"Then you do it," Patty said.

"No way," Valerie said. "It's disgusting."

● ● ●

The slingshot guys were having a powwow in one of their designated areas. Scott and I crept up behind the group, ducking behind a couple of trees.

"I can't come up with anything," one said.

"Why do we have to prove we're a benefit to society? We just want to be able to use slingshots," another said.

"Look, I don't agree with this ruling any more than you do, but we have to think of something. We have to show we have some purpose. Now everybody think!" Ben, their leader, ordered.

They all bowed their heads and squinted their eyes shut,

clearly trying to squeeze every ounce of intelligence out of their brains.

"What are we here for?" Ben said. "What's our purpose?"

"Protection. We're here so that Kidsborians can feel safe in their homes."

"Right. Protection. But from what?"

They all looked at each other, and then one said, "Bears?"

"How can we prove that, though?"

"Man, if only a bear would attack or something."

"Oh, that would be perfect."

"Maybe we could lure one here. Put out some food or something."

"I've never seen any bears around here."

"We'll have to go deeper in the woods."

"Yeah. There's tons of bears out there."

"That's it. We go find a bear, shoot it with a slingshot, then drag it back here and tell everybody we saved them from certain death."

"Yeah!"

"That's it!"

"Let's do it!"

They picked up their slingshots and marched onward, heads held high. They all high-fived each other, whooping and hollering as they headed deeper into the woods as a group. Scott was holding his hand over his mouth to keep from laughing.

Suddenly, one of the slingshotters stopped. "Wait a minute."

"What?"

"We're gonna shoot a bear?"

They all halted, and it suddenly dawned on them what they had decided to do. They exchanged frightened looks.

"We can do this," Ben said. No one else seemed convinced, but no one wanted to admit his fear. They moved on into the woods, though there was no more hollering, and their steps weren't quite so quick.

● ● ●

Scott and I were pretending to casually walk past the farmers' garden. We slowed our steps to overhear Mark and the Clean Up Kidsboro group having a feud with the farmers. "What is that?" Mark said to farmer/doctor James. "What are you putting on your plants?"

"It's bug killer," James replied.

"That stuff pollutes the environment. You can't use it."

"If we don't use this, the bugs'll eat everything. These beetle things are all over the place."

"I guess they're gonna have a feast then."

"Sorry, but you'll have to fight pollution somewhere else. This is our garden, and it's got to look a lot better than this in three days if we're gonna keep our funding."

"You keep using that death spray, and you won't have a garden to show."

"What do you mean?"

"You put one drop of it on your plants, and we'll rip 'em all out by the roots."

"What?"

• • •

We passed by the feminists, and they had begun work on the latrine walls. I imagined they were doing this to put off having to dig, which was much more offensive. They had built a frame of wood, and it looked rather good.

• • •

Scott and I were kneeling behind some tall bushes, watching Melissa and the animal rights group attempt to train their dogs to pick up rocks in the middle of Kidsboro's main street and take them to the creek. Apparently, this would be the way they would show that their dogs benefited Kidsboro—by getting rid of dangerous rocks that people could trip over.

The trainers weren't having much success. "Come on, Tornado," an owner said to his terrier. "Pick up the rock. Pick it up, boy." The owner looked around to see if anyone was watching, then got down on all fours and demonstrated the technique to his dog. He picked up a rock in his mouth and carried it away, then turned around to see if his dog would do it. At this point, Scott and I were both stuffing our fists in our mouths to keep from bursting out laughing.

The dog just looked at his owner as if to say, "Well, if *you're* going to pick up the rocks, then there's no sense in me doing it. You can take them to the creek. And while you're there, would you mind filling my water dish? It's kind of a long walk."

• • •

Two days later there was panic in the air. None of the groups were making much progress with their assignments, and they had only 24 hours left. I was nearby the designated slingshot area as the guys returned from another unsuccessful bear-hunting trip. They came back with a couple of dead crickets.

"But crickets are gross," one of them said. "They spit this tobacco-like stuff, and they jump on you. The government should pay us big bucks to rid our town of these pesky marauders of freedom." The rest of the guys weren't buying it. They must have known that two dead crickets were not enough to pass the test. I found out later that it had taken 14 shots from four different people to hit the first cricket with their slingshots. The other one they had just stepped on.

● ● ●

The feminists were holding a six-person rally at the meeting hall pavilion to psyche themselves up for digging the hole. The walls were complete, but they had yet to break ground with their shovels. Scott and I peeked in.

Valerie was at the front, her fist waving madly. "We can do this, girls!" Wild cheers. "We are entering a new age where there is no difference between boys and girls!" More applause. "An age where we can do anything boys can do! I have a dream! I have a dream that one day boys will be cleaning the kitchen cabinets, and girls will be choosing the president's cabinet. I have a dream that girls will be found within the capitol walls and boys in the shopping malls!" The girls were now in a frenzy. "I have a dream that one day there will be girls and boys standing side by side, kings and queens, dresses and jeans, Chrises and Christines, using all their means, to dig latrines!"

Valerie had them going crazy, and didn't want to lose them. She grabbed a shovel and raised it above her head. "This is the symbol of girls now! We use shovels! We dig dirt! We do construction! We get dirty!" They all raised their shovels.

Valerie reached up and pulled off her earrings. "These are no longer a symbol of us!" she said, and threw the earrings into the grass behind her. Another girl joined her and started raising her own symbols in the air. She picked up a pair of pantyhose and threw them away. Another girl threw her purse about 30 feet. They'd obviously been told beforehand to bring all the symbols of girlhood because everyone seemed to have something to throw away—jewelry, acrylic nails, perfume, and makeup.

Patty raised up a can of hairspray and shot it out into the air, waving it to show the stream. Just then, Mark, head of Clean Up Kidsboro, flew out of a nearby bush. He had obviously been watching them to make sure they finished the bathroom. But now, I had a feeling he thought the feminists had gone too far.

"Hey! Stop that!" he yelled. Most of the girls ignored him, including Patty, who continued spraying. "Those are harmful chemicals!" he protested.

She continued to ignore him. "Stop spraying!" he yelled, jumping up and snatching the can from her hand. Some of the girls finally noticed that there was a boy present, and their frenzy came to an abrupt halt. "What are you people doing?" Mark shouted. "You're killing us! My organization is relying on you. You're supposed to be digging a latrine, not spraying deadly chemicals in the air!"

"We're just about to dig," Patty said.

"Well, get started, then! You've only got 24 hours, or we lose our funding!"

"How about it, girls?" Valerie shouted, trying to regain the momentum.

"Yeah!" they shouted.

"Then let's go!" she shouted, raising her shovel in the air. Each girl grabbed her shovel. Like angry villagers ready to lynch somebody, they marched out to the latrine construction site, shouting as they went. Mark followed them to see that the job would actually be done this time. Scott and I went along too.

The feminists all circled around the spot where the bathroom was going to be built. "Let's make a toilet, girls!" They all cheered, but something about the words *toilet girls* hit them. A couple glanced around and could see that there were several boys in the distance, watching them carefully as they prepared to break ground. I think each of them had their own vision of walking down the halls of the school, with boys all around them pointing and saying, "There goes one of the toilet girls." Somehow this vision seemed to drain their enthusiasm. Valerie stood with her shovel poised above the ground, ready to strike down on the earth. Then she looked around and saw more boys watching her from across the creek. She scanned the faces of her followers and realized that they had lost their fervor. They suddenly wanted their makeup and hairspray back.

"Come on!" Mark said, noticing the sudden change of attitude. "Dig! Come on! It's only a hole!"

Valerie handed him the shovel. "Then you do it."

"No way; that's disgusting."

• • •

James marched over to where the animal rights group was busy trying to train their cats to rake leaves. One cat carried a small rake on its back like a plow horse. *This is animal rights?* I asked myself.

James was irate. "Your dogs are destroying our garden," he shouted.

"How?"

"You've trained them to pick up rocks and take them to the creek, and now they're doing it to my unripe tomatoes!"

"Really?" one of them said with glee. They were excited that the dogs were using what they'd learned.

"Keep your dogs out of my garden."

"Well, if you haven't noticed," the animal lover replied, "we have laws now that say that animals can roam freely, just like humans. The dogs can go anywhere they want."

"So, you're not gonna keep them out?"

"Nope."

"All right, then." James left. He walked away so quickly it was obvious that he had a plan. Scott and I followed quietly behind him.

He went to see the slingshotters. "I have a job for you," he said.

Their eyes lit up. "What?"

"I want to keep the dogs out of our garden. I'll hire you to stand guard. If any of those dogs come near it, open fire."

"Really?" the slingshotters said in unison. They huddled up. "This is our chance. We can show we're useful to the farmers." They all nodded in agreement and broke the huddle.

"We'll do it," they said. James smiled.

● ● ●

Later that day, the slingshotters had the garden surrounded, waiting for the dogs to make one false move. It was like a police stakeout. They sat there for an hour without a single animal in sight, their trigger fingers itching to fire away.

Suddenly, one of the slingshotters got hit. A stray nut from out of nowhere pelted him on the back of the head. He turned around. It was Melissa, holding a slingshot of her own.

"What are you doing?" the slingshotter asked, his buddies giving up their positions and gathering around him.

"How does that feel?" Melissa said. "What if the dogs just suddenly started shooting at you? Doesn't feel so good, does it?"

All at once, three more animal rights people appeared from behind the trees. They all had slingshots. Melissa signaled them forward. "It's hunting season, boys." They advanced on the slingshotters with an entire arsenal of nuts and hard objects in their pockets. The slingshotters, who had left their weapons at their posts, backed away and started to run. The animal rights people ran after them, shooting at will. The slingshotters retreated into the woods until we couldn't see them anymore.

NINE

TIME'S UP

A MISCHIEVOUS GRIN CROSSED my face as I headed into Kidsboro the next morning. The 72 hours was up for all the special-interest groups, and I could already tell that some of them were going to fall short. I passed the garden on my way to the office; the bugs and animals had destroyed it. It didn't even resemble a garden anymore, it looked more like a greenhouse that had been bombed. One of the farmers was sitting beside it and waved sheepishly at me. He was caressing a perfect unripe tomato. Maybe it was the only one left.

Along the way, I saw that garbage was strewn everywhere, down the main street all the way across the creek and into Bettertown. Scott was noticing it as well.

"What happened here?" I asked him.

"Corey overslept, and the animals had a party." This was the garbageman who had just gotten a raise because he thought he deserved as much money as the mayor and the chief of police.

The city council met in the meeting hall; we were all curious as to what we were going to see today.

The slingshotters came in first. They dropped three dead crickets and a snail on the table. Half-heartedly, Ben said, "We have to rid the woods of these." He looked at us to see if there was even a hint that we were taking him seriously. He gave up in about five seconds. "Never mind. Let's go," he said, and the others followed.

Clean Up Kidsboro was next. Mark stood in front of me with all the pride he could muster. The rest of his group stood behind him.

"Let's see here," I said, reading over their contract. "You were supposed to make Kidsboro litter-free."

Mark raised his eyebrows and chuckled under his breath. "It was the dogs."

"Part of your job was to keep Kidsboro clean, despite dogs running around," I said.

"Yeah. We know." Mark turned and left.

• • •

Melissa and the animal rights people strolled in with just one dog.

"Melissa, we asked that you make sure these animals had jobs. Could you please show us what they're doing now?"

"Well, Bowzer here is going to show you how he can deliver things directly to someone's door."

"Really?" I said, looking forward to this demonstration.

"Okay, boy," she said to the basset hound, who lay prostrate on the ground. "Take this ball to Nelson's house." She handed him a ball, but he failed to grab it. She dropped the ball on the ground in front of him. He sniffed it. It was obvious that he was one of the dogs that had gone through the garbage and had such a full stomach that he had no desire to get up.

"Come on, boy. Come on, Bowzer." She glanced at me sheepishly. I tried to hide my grin. Bowzer burped and closed his eyes.

"They just need more training," she said.

"I've been around dogs. I know dogs. Training a dog not to tear through garbage is like training a fish not to swim," I said. Scott snickered, and Nelson elbowed him.

● ● ●

The farmers came in with the remains of a watermelon plant. It had been chewed through by beetles. "I could almost taste this watermelon," James said and laid it down on the table in front of us.

● ● ●

Valerie came in with her shovel. She was covered in dirt from head to toe. "You got your bathroom. But do me a favor. Don't give us any more government jobs," she said, spearing the ground with the shovel and walking away.

The city council members exchanged looks and started chuckling.

"We gotta do this again sometime," Scott said.

"Absolutely," Nelson said.

"Next time, I'll bring the popcorn," Jill said.

Alice just smiled with her arms crossed. For Alice, who rarely even smiled, much less laughed, this was like rolling on the floor.

We all laughed and talked for 20 minutes or so, and then remembered that we had jobs to do. Mainly, we had to vote to change the budget plan to exclude the groups who failed to pass their tests. It was unanimous. The budget would be amended.

● ● ●

I couldn't really get any work done on the budget when I got back to my office. I was too distracted thinking about how this was going to benefit Kidsboro. The special-interest groups had lost their funding, taxes were back to normal, and Nelson would be able to hire his employees back. I sat at my desk with my hands folded behind my head, very proud of myself.

There was a knock at my door, and Lauren came in. I had completely forgotten that I had given her an assignment, and that it was due. My glee suddenly turned sour because I knew I was going to have to fire her.

"Mr. Mayor?" she said, stepping in anxiously.

"Lauren, come in." She did, and then she sat down. I swallowed a lump in my throat and asked, "How did you do?"

"I don't know. I hope I did okay."

"You finished it?"

"Yes."

She handed me her work. It was hardbound like a textbook and much thicker than the city charter I had given her. I opened it, and my chin dropped to the floor. Inside were beautiful computer graphics, illustrations, and big ornate fonts. Written in gold calligraphy on the first page, were the

words: *The City Charter of Kidsboro*. It almost made me weep.
On the sides were category dividers—the divisions were perfect: judicial, legislative, and executive branches of government, just like in the Constitution of the United States.

There was a table of contents on page three, dividing up the book into sections, such as the government; the courts; elections; rights of citizens; selection of citizens—every word spelled correctly, every punctuation mark in the right place.

It was beautiful.

"Lauren . . . this is fantastic!"

"Really? You like it?"

"I can't believe this. You did a great job! How many hours did you spend?"

"All day every day. I've slept a total of seven hours over the last two nights."

"But, why?"

She seemed stunned by the question. "Because I love this job. I love working here. I love . . . working with you."

I smiled, and we looked at each other for a long moment. Even with an average of three-and-a-half hours of sleep the past two nights, she was radiant.

We were interrupted by a knock on the door. "Come in," I said.

It was Jill. "Oh, Lauren. Hi." She looked at me. I think she thought I was in the middle of firing Lauren. "Oh, I'm sorry. I guess you're . . . I'd better get going."

"No. Wait, Jill. I was just about to send Lauren home to get some sleep," I said.

"Thank you," Lauren said, smiling.

"Oh. I see," Jill said, then looked at Lauren sympatheti-
cally. "Hey, I'm sorry about . . . you know . . . But with the
taxes . . ."

"Jill, Lauren did a great job on the charter."

"What?"

"Here."

She looked at the charter and her jaw dropped even farther than mine had. "This is great."

"Thanks," Lauren said.

"Why don't you go home now?" I said.

"Okay. Thanks. I'll see you first thing tomorrow."

"Bright and early," I called after her. She left.

"You're really gonna keep her on?" Jill asked, shutting
the book.

"Look at what she did."

"One project. Big deal. Can she be consistent?"

"I don't know. But we're gonna see."

"Yeah, I guess we will."

"Jill," I said, "What's your problem with her? You've
been really focused on getting her out of here. Why?"

"I don't have a problem with her," she said.

I smiled at her because I knew she was lying. She always
looked over my shoulder instead of at my face when she was
telling me something that she knew was untrue.

She smiled back because she knew I knew. "Maybe I just
don't think she's good enough for you."

"She's my assistant, not my fiancée."

"Maybe I can sense a little office romance budding
between you two."

"And why would that bother you?"

She chuckled and looked away from me. "You deserve a good speller."

"Yeah. You're right. I do."

● ● ●

Dear Dad,

One of my favorite memories of you is when you taught me how to make a soapbox derby car. You were so set on me learning to do it right that you made me repeat all of your instructions, and you had me do all the work myself so that I could get a feel for it. I never told you this, but I had no interest in soapbox derby cars. I didn't care about making one, and I've never made one since. I've probably forgotten all you told me. But I always loved learning from you. You were a good teacher.

And I hadn't realized how much I missed listening to you teach until last week. Last week I made an unpopular decision in Kidsboro, and I had half the people in town hating me. A lot of groups lost their government funding because of me, and everybody was pretty sore. They might not like me right now, but you taught me that at least they respect me now. And they trust me. I'll try very hard not to break that trust.

Anyway, I just wanted to let you know that you are still teaching me. Even if you're behind bars, miles away, you're still showing me what it takes to be a man.

I would be lying if I told you I wasn't glad you're behind bars. I am finally able to sleep at night. You deserve to be in prison, and I don't know if I'll ever be able to forgive you for what you did to Mom and me. But there's also a part of me that knows you're still my dad and wishes that we could one day be a family again. I know that's not likely, but I do want you to know that there were times when you were a good father. I still love that part of you very much.

I'll see you again sometime.

Your son,

Jim

THE END

FOCUS ON THE FAMILY®

At Focus on the Family, we work to help you really get to know Jesus and equip you to change your world for Him.

We realize the struggles you face are different from your parents' or your little brother's, so we've developed a lot of resources specifically to help you live boldly for Christ, no matter what's happening in your life.

Besides exciting novels, we have Web sites, magazines, booklets, and devotionals...all dealing with the stuff you care about.

Breakaway®
Teen guys
breakawaymag.com

Focus on the Family Magazines

We know you want to stay up-to-date on the latest in your world—but it's hard to find information on entertainment, trends, and relevant issues that doesn't drag you down. It's even harder to find magazines that deliver what you want and need from a Christ-honoring perspective.

That's why we created *Breakaway* (for teen guys), *Brio* (for teen girls), and *Clubhouse* (for tweens, ages 8 to 12). So, don't be left out—sign up today!

Brio®
Teen girls 13 to 15
briomag.com

Focus on the Family
Clubhouse™
Tweens ages 8 to 12
clubhousemagazine.com

Adventures in ODYSSEY
Weekly Radio Show
whitsend.org

 Phone toll free: (800) A-FAMILY (232-6459)
In Canada, call toll free: (800) 661-9800

BP06XTN

More Great Resources
from Focus on the Family®

Adventures in Odyssey® Novels
by Paul McCusker | Three book series | Paperback
Uncover Odyssey's past—and all-new stories with your
favorite characters—in this prequel series! Ever wondered
how the Imagination Station was invented? What's the
story behind Jimmy's salvation? You'll get answers in these
exciting tales that follow the adventures of Whit and
many others. Each megabook contains four novels in one!

Passages Fiction Series
by Paul McCusker | Six book series | Paperback
Follow new friends from Odyssey as they stumble into the
land of Marus, where two moons light the night sky and
visitors from Odyssey discover strange new powers. Pas-
sages books begin in Odyssey and transport you to a fan-
tasy land, where belief in God becomes the adventure of a
lifetime. Recommended for ages 10 and up.

Growing Up Super Average
by comedian Bob Smiley and Jesse Florea | Paperback
Since first showing up in *Clubhouse* magazine, Average
Boy has given readers a funny look at all the important
stuff in life. Now *Growing Up Super Average*, with hilari-
ous new stories, will help you laugh *and* be super average
where it matters: getting along with your friends, handling
money, knowing God, and lots more.

FOR MORE INFORMATION

Online:
Log on to www.family.org
In Canada, log on to www.focusonthefamily.ca.

Phone:
Call toll free: (800) A-FAMILY
In Canada, call toll free: (800) 661-9800.

BP06XP1

THE LAST CHANCE DETECTIVES ®

Their town is Ambrosia . . . their headquarters is a vintage B-17 bomber . . . and they are The Last Chance Detectives . . . four ordinary kids who team up to solve mysteries no one else can be bothered with. Now, for the first time, the three best-selling episodes in the series are available in one DVD gift set.

Request this collector's edition set by calling the number below. And see if you can crack the cases of *Mystery Lights of Navajo Mesa*, *Legend of the Desert Bigfoot*, and *Escape from Fire Lake*.

And for the latest audio exploits of The Last Chance Detectives, call that same number. Request your copy of *The Day Ambrosia Stood Still*, *Mystery of the Lost Voices*, and *Last Flight of the Dragon Lady*.

Phone toll free: (800) A-FAMILY (232-6459)